THE DAY OF MURDER

The body had been there a week before it was discovered. Detective Superintendent Townley and Sergeant Newman have a houseful of suspects. But who savagely killed the promiscuous woman in her flat? The time of death is narrowed to a few hours on the Sunday morning, which points to the only visitor to the house at that time — the parish priest. Yet there are eight suspects in total . . . and Townley and Newman will identify the guilty party before the day is out.

BRIAN BEARSHAW

THE DAY OF MURDER

Complete and Unabridged

LINFORD
Leicester

First published in Great Britain
by Robert Hale Limited
London

First Linford Edition
published 2006
by arrangement with
Robert Hale Limited
London

British Library CIP Data

Bearshaw, Brian, *1932* –
The day of murder.—Large print ed.—
Linford mystery library
1. Murder—Investigation—England—Fiction
2. Police—England—Fiction 3. Detective and
mystery stories 4. Large type books
I. Title
823.9′14 [F]

ISBN 1–84617–567–4

Published by
F. A. Thorpe (Publishing)
Anstey, Leicestershire

Set by Words & Graphics Ltd.
Anstey, Leicestershire
Printed and bound in Great Britain by
T. J. International Ltd., Padstow, Cornwall

This book is printed on acid-free paper

To Max Reese,
for a timely push at Tunbridge Wells

1

By the time the police arrived, the body was clearly in its first stages of putrefaction.

The skin had taken on its waxy yellow hue, a sickeningly sweet colour, slightly heightened by the green stain that had appeared on the lower part of the abdomen.

The muscles of the face had relaxed and the corpse had assumed the classic appearance, staring eyes and a gaping mouth, the look of the frightened child awakened from a bad dream.

Rigor mortis, which starts in the neck muscles a few hours after death and which spreads to the other muscles within a few hours more, had worn off. The body was relaxed again.

Livid spots, often mistaken for bruising, had appeared on the back, as the blood which had spurted out like a spring when the bread knife had sunk into the body again and again, had run into the lowest parts of the body. The blood, no longer circulating the veins and arteries, had settled, at rest for ever.

Detective Superintendent Robert Townley walked into the flat of the murdered woman almost an hour after the main body of policemen, headed by his sergeant, Stuart Newman, had arrived at the scene. Now only Newman remained.

Townley had been on his weekly visit to his 92-year-old grandfather 20 miles away in Blowton, and had just been ready to leave for home when a patrol car from the local force had called to tell him of the murder.

Townley was one of life's working-class men with a middle-class outlook. He thought of himself as a professional man with a rank of superiority that gave him good claims to being middle class.

'My father and my father's father and every father before him might have belonged to the working-class,' he once said. 'But they'll not put me in that bloody category.'

Certainly he strove hard for recognition

among the middle classes. He knew all the latest drinks. He had advanced from whisky and Canada dry, through gin and tonic, vodka and bitter lemon, bacardi and coke, to pernod and water.

He drank a glass of wine with his dinner — unambitious £1.50 a litre wine — brandy with his coffee, and liver salts before bed.

He drove a Rover car, his wife had a Mini, he holidayed abroad every summer, was a member of the Rotary Club, attended mass wherever possible, and voted Liberal. Hell, now that IS middle class.

Townley was really nothing more than an inspector. But opportunity had come his way, good luck had come to him just when it mattered, misgivings were overlooked — as were one or two better policemen with lower social aspirations — and he achieved a status that would never have been his in industry. He was a somebody in the town of Rosedale, Detective Superintendent Somebody, that nobody could deny.

His stature matched his position. He

was 6ft 4in tall, weighed nearly 15st, and his years in the police force had taught him that a man with pride in himself was a man indeed. He stood erect, a Grenadier Guard from the well-shod heels of his boots to the top of his shining, slippery bald head.

At least, it would have been shining and slippery if it had faced the world. But Townley had his appearance to think of. He wore a wig. No, better than that, a hair piece. After all, a man is entitled to the odd vanity, even at a cost of £118.75. Plus V.A.T.

Townley breezed in through the open door, took one glance at the blood and the body, and experienced that nauseating feeling that overtook him every time he saw a body that had died with some element of violence.

His reaction was always the same. Detective Sergeant Newman knew it off by heart. It was like watching the replay of England's World Cup win over West Germany at Wembley. He had seen it so many times he knew every stride, every syllable.

Townley gaped, his face a temporary repeat of that on the body, took off his corduroy, captain-like cap, ran his hand through £118.75 worth of hairs — plus V.A.T. — and muttered: 'Holy grandfather.'

The whole force knew Townley visited his grandfather, who from all accounts was the most unholy, ungodly man in the whole of the North of England, and Newman assumed that this suppressed oath stemmed in some unlikely way from the old man.

Townley then quickly looked round the room, ignoring the repulsive, lifeless form on the bed, more false looking and hideous than anything in Madame Tussaud's.

To all appearances, Townley was taking in his surroundings, soaking up the atmosphere, casting around for clues. In reality, he was making damn sure he didn't vomit all over the blood-stained carpet.

It was always like this at the beginning. A few seconds, and he'd be as normal as the day itself. Except for the slaver of sweat that formed on his forehead. Just below the join.

This was the living room of the flat. The body lay on the comfortable, springy couch, and before he had taken his eyes away from it, Townley had noticed the stab wounds, about a dozen of them, none higher than the collar bone, none lower than the naval.

The inevitable television set stood alongside, and next to that, the fireplace and the Miser Gas fire, one of the blessings of the modern life.

Above the fireplace was a Breugel picture, Hunters in the Snow, stark and white and cold, a compelling painting. Perhaps somebody had stepped down from it into this room, bored by the pointless chase over the cold Flemish hills, drawn by the fire and enflamed by the naked woman. Try telling that to the Chief Constable . . .

Through the window, Townley could just make out the edge of the garden below, the tall, wrought-iron gates that led out on to the quiet Woodland Road, led in to the tarmacadammed drive that wandered completely round the detached house which had been transformed into a block of six flats.

Two coffee cups still stood on the low, home-made table, the Sunday Chronicle, still looking clean and unopened, lying undisturbed beside them.

Two easy chairs, one with a woman's magazine lying on it, two stand chairs, a standard lamp, a small desk littered with letters, circulars and old newspapers, made up the room.

Except, that is, for the bread knife, the killer's weapon, stretched out on the once-immaculate white rug like the cat in front of the fire.

It was almost entirely covered with blood. Townley's gaze rested on it a few seconds. He was nearly ready for a second, better look at the body.

'Just one set of prints,' said Newman, anticipating the question. 'Probably the deceased's, I'm having them checked out.'

'Only one!' exclaimed Townley. 'On both cups.'

'That's right sir, just one. The other

cup was completely clean. Must have been wiped.'

Townley's eyes came back to the body. Female, naked, apparently stabbed as she lay. Raven-haired and slender. Close her eyes and mouth and she might even have been beautiful. The body looked ready for love.

Whatever it had been ready for, it had not been the angry, deep wounds that covered the chest, violent signs of a raging anger. Maybe madness.

The couch had soaked up much of the woman's blood, which had spurted on to the white-emulsioned wall, on to the screen of the television set, and helped to make more patterns on a carpet thick with floral designs.

Newman waited for the Superintendent to settle once more on the body. 'A bloody mess sir,' he said without passion.

Newman was not swearing. He never swore. A sign of weakness, he believed. There were enough words in the English language to cover any situation. ANY situation. Swearing simply covered an enormous void in a human being's vocabulary. No, Newman was not swearing. Just being literal in accordance with the facts.

Townley thankfully took his eyes away again from the horror and settled them on Newman, on his strict, severe hair-cut, short back and sides they used to call it at the barber's.

'You could say that, sergeant. Mmmm, you could say that. Right, well what do we know?'

Newman took out his notebook from his jacket pocket, found the relevant page, and launched forth.

'Female, aged between 25 and 30, known as Doreen Masters. Bank clerk in town with Barclays, single, an assortment of boy friends, friendly sort of woman, but did not seem to need close friends. Nobody she seemed particularly fond of or close to, man or woman. Body discovered this morning by the window cleaner, one George Hart, one of the flat occupants who made this his job every second Saturday.

'Subject to the post mortem, it seems she must have been killed some time last

Sunday. The Sunday Chronicle from that day was in the flat, which was locked, all the other papers from Monday to today, six of them, were lying behind the door.

'There was no accumulation of milk at the door to warn anybody earlier as she always collected whatever she needed from the grocer's shop across the road.'

Townley interrupted. He liked putting in a word here and there. Showed superiority, rank. As if anybody could have found all that out, but what about the important parts.

'Did nobody at Barclays Bank think it unusual for her not to appear at work . . . all week?' he asked. 'Surely somebody could have called.'

Newman lifted his head from his notebook. It was a boss's prerogative to put in his twopennyworth. It didn't worry him. He'd only had an hour start on the 'Super,' but he thought he had pieced together a good enough description. For starters anyway.

'I haven't had time to check that sir.' Newman knew better than to wait for an observation on that. With hardly a breath he picked up from where he had been so rudely interrupted.

'There are ten stab wounds in the body, the only obvious signs of violence.'

Townley couldn't resist. 'I'd say those ten were more than enough.'

Newman sighed at his own stupidity. 'I meant to say that there were no signs of a struggle, no indication that she had been knocked about before. She had laid her clothes out tidily in the bedroom and by all appearances had gone into the living room voluntarily.'

Townley tugged at a few pennysworth of his crowning glory, replaced them in precisely their exact positions, and gazed out of the window.

'So we can assume that she knew the person who attacked her. Sexual intercourse had either taken place or was about to be conducted when the assailant struck.'

'I hadn't taken it that far, sir,' said Newman. 'A woman doesn't always take her clothes off just to have sex relations.'

'I do,' said the Superintendent. 'And my wife does. Your remark would have some substance if she were alone. But she wasn't. She had a man with her, quite clearly, and she hadn't taken off her clothes, laid them down neatly, just to switch on the bloody telly, had she?'

'It could have been a woman sir . . . '

'Oh, come on Newman,' said Townley impatiently. There were no first name-terms with Detective Superintendent Somebody. The ranks had to be kept in their place. Beneath.

'You said earlier that she had assorted boy friends, so it seems we can rule out lesbianism. Just about. And she's hardly likely to get in the nude for a Sunday cuppa with a girl friend, is she?'

Newman didn't persist. If the occasion arose, the 'Super' would change his mind quicker than a politician. In any case he had a choice piece of information on the way that would eliminate that train of thought. He continued.

'Three of the five other flats are empty at the moment, but I have spoken to Mr. Hart, the window cleaner, and an elderly lady, a Mrs . . . ' Newman squinted at his own writing, making sure he had the name right . . . 'Gladys Victoria Shuttleworth.'

Townley couldn't suppress a giggle. At times like these he was like a schoolgirl. When his fancy was tickled he didn't smile or smirk, he didn't roar his head off or collapse in a heap like a Styx cartoon. He tittered like a fourth-former who had just heard the one about the boy and the bath-tap for the first time.

'Quite a mouthful, eh sergeant?' said his superior between cackles.

Newman stifled another sigh. He'd laugh the other side of his face when he told him.

'Mr. Hart says the last time he saw the deceased was last Saturday, sir, when he cleaned her windows.'

'You said he only cleaned them every second Saturday, sergeant.'

'Miss Masters he managed EVERY week, sir. I gather that if his luck was in and the gas fire was turned up, he just might see her in her nothings.'

Townley giggled again. 'Probably cleaned the old lady's once a bloody year then, I suppose.'

Newman was appalled. Here they were, a savage murder on their hands, the body six feet away, and Superintendent Townley simpering as if he were looking for a Peeping Tom.

'Mr. Hart,' Newman continued, 'was sure it was Saturday and cannot say much about Sunday as he was away fishing all day.'

Now he'd show him. 'But Mrs. Shuttleworth remembers seeing one man here on Sunday. She remembers particularly because she went to collect her milk from the door ready to mash her potatoes. Puts milk in her mashed potatoes,' said Newman, as if the statement needed elaborating.

'Oh get on man,' said Townley. 'I'm not interested in Gladys Shuttleworth's culinary secrets. Did she know the fellow?'

'Yes indeed, sir, she knew him well. In fact she had seen him earlier that same morning.'

'Where, Newman, where?'

'In church, sir, at eight o'clock mass. It was the priest!'

2

'THE PRIEST!' Townley bellowed. 'THE PRIEST?'

Newman could hardly suppress a smug smile of satisfaction. He had dropped his bomb and the Superintendent had blown up. Just as he knew he would.

Townley quickly subsided after his outburst. After all, what did it mean? Nothing more than that Mrs. Shuttleworth, en route for the milk, had seen one man on the day of the murder. And a priest at that. There could have been a thousand other men in the house that day that she hadn't seen.

'Which priest is it?' he asked.

'Father Johnston. Father Joseph Johnston. He's at St. Aidan's Church up the road, fairly new, came here about 18 months ago. One of these new brooms, forever sweeping out the old, and blowing in new ideas.'

'Hang on a minute, Newman,' said

Townley. 'Does Mrs. Shuttleworth know for sure that Father Johnston was heading for this flat?'

'No sir. Mrs. Shuttleworth has one of the two flats on the ground floor, and all she can say for sure is that Father Johnston went upstairs.'

'Which meant he could have been going to any one of four flats,' said Townley.

'Quite right sir. Except we do know for sure that he actually came to this door.'

'How do we know that?'

'Well sir, among the newspapers at the back of the door was an electric bill, and right at the bottom . . . a letter to Miss Masters from Father Johnston. Here it is.'

Townley grabbed the letter out of his sergeant's hands. It was in a foolscap envelope, addressed to 'Miss Doreen Masters.' The Superintendent took out a sheet of notepaper and began to read aloud.

He enjoyed reading aloud. Nothing delighted him more than having to give evidence in court, any court, and on the odd occasion he was asked to address

Mothers Unions and Young Wives he positively purred with supreme pleasure. Really, he believed, his true vocation was to have been a public speaker in some higher role . . . a Member of Parliament, or a television news reader perhaps. Or a priest . . .

' 'Doreen' — that's a mite familiar for a priest to a woman with assorted boy friends, eh Newman? 'Doreen, I called to see you this morning, but unfortunately I could get no reply. I assume you were out. At least I hope you weren't avoiding me. Sorry I missed you. I'll call again. Father Johnston.'

'Pity he didn't sign himself 'Your loving Joe' eh? Still, this is something to go on Newman. I think it's time we paid a visit to Father Johnston and found out what he was doing here the day a young woman was savagely stabbed to death. You've had the routines taken care of, prints, photographs . . . '

Newman interrupted him. 'Of course, sir. All taken care of.'

'Right, then you go and see this parish priest, Newman. I'm going across the road to the grocer's to see when was the last time Miss Masters collected milk. How much was there in the flat by the way?'

'I don't know sir. I'll just have a look in the kitchen. See what there is.'

As Newman left for the kitchen, Townley again looked round the room. He noticed in the ash tray that as well as innumerable cigarette ends, there were the remains of a small cigar — what did they call them? Some fancy name he couldn't recall.

The coffee cups still had the remains of black coffee, and some had spilled on to the table.

Townley idly picked up the newspaper, last Sunday's newspaper. The Sunday Chronicle. One of the Sunday sexies, a single man's paper perhaps, but not usually a woman's. He must remember to find out what time this had been delivered.

Townley turned to the back page. He wished he hadn't. There, again, in cold print, was the Cup defeat of his favourite team, Manchester United. He wasn't sure why he had become attached to United. He hardly ever got the chance to watch them, and heaven knows why he did, because he hated big crowds. But there was a magic about them, a magnetism that drew Townley so that he felt part of their victories, and just as squashed when they were beaten. He would certainly never watch his own town team, waffling about in the middle of the Fourth Division, and anyway, it was only 12 miles to Manchester. And he did like the city.

But at least United's catastrophe was not all across the back page of this newspaper. They'd settled for Newcastle for some reason best known to themselves. 'The workings of newspapers are way beyond me,' he said to himself, a phrase he was fond of repeating out loud whenever anybody — his wife particularly — asked him to explain something from the newspaper that he knew exactly nothing about.

He looked around for the United report and found it, across two columns, in the bottom half of the page. At least, it's out of the way there, he thought. He was just about to relive the horror when Newman came back into the room.

'Two bottles left, sir. One of them empty and washed, the other with just a drop left in the bottom.'

'Right,' said Townley. 'Well, I'm off to the grocer's, then I'll see the dear Mrs. Shuttleworth, and anybody else who might be in the place. You can tell them to remove the body — just as quickly as they like because I'll be coming back soon — but to leave everything else as it is. I want another look at this little lot. Tell Brooks I want the post mortem report double quick, too. Now you get off to the priest. Find out what he knows about 'Doreen', how often he's been seeing her, what time he came here last Sunday, how long he stayed, and why the hell he wasn't at mass.'

Newman bristled. Townley regularly had this effect upon him. One day HE might explode. Why the devil couldn't the great Superintendent at least allow you to use one ounce of initiative? Still, it wasn't just him. He did it with everybody in the

Force. He never sent anybody away, simply telling them to interview. Oh, no, he had to list the questions for you. Someday he'll be asking for a secretary to go along with him to take the questions down in shorthand and rattle them off on a portable typewriter for the officer to take with him. Newman headed for the door without another word. He reached for the handle.

'And find out if there's any other women he goes to see regularly, young women, and whether he's in the habit of calling them by their first names. And if his housekeeper's under 35 I want to know about it,' he shouted.

Newman hadn't moved for a few seconds. He remained like a statue, his hand on the door handle, his eyes firmly fixed to the door panel near the handle.

Without turning, Newman spoke, quietly, concealing the cynicism that was itching to pour out of him. 'Maybe I should ask him, sir, when he last had sexual intercourse or when he last saw a naked woman.'

He had veiled his sarcasm well. It was

lost on the Superintendent. 'You might just as well lad,' he said. Newman cringed. He really was talking down to him now, rank was showing, the Superintendent addressing the Sergeant.

'Ay, you might just as well. They're only flesh and fat like me and you, lad. And who knows, maybe they have the same flaming passions as you and me, now and again.'

Newman waited no longer. He opened the door and as he was closing it behind him, caught the parting words . . . 'Well, me anyway,' and that infernal giggle.

Townley was waiting no longer. He'd seen enough of that gaping, staring, rotting body. He needed some cigarettes and a breath of fresh air. Newman would organise the body's removal. He was good at organisation was Newman. Not good to let him know though. He was the sort of fellow you had to sit on, to push, to keep at. Never let them think they were any good. No good at all. Or they might try to rise above their station.

He followed close behind Newman, but out on the landing there was no sign of the Sergeant. Good, keep at them. Just like a bayonet up the backside. It made them move.

He went down stairs into the good-sized hall. There was a door on either side, presumably into each of the two ground-floor flats, one of them the inimitable Gladys Shuttleworth. He'd save her until later.

He turned the lock on the front door and walked out on to the drive which wound past a large lawn on its way to the impressive doubled-gated entrance at Woodland Road.

Rosedale was a thriving, industrial town, a population approaching 100,000, typically Lancashire, but unfortunately losing so much of what had given it its character. Mills had closed, the chimneys would one day all be gone, clogs and shawls were already things of the past, even cobbled streets were frowned on.

But the hard times of the depression had gone, and people had money to spend. They were still thrifty, they still liked the bustle and appeal and competition of the market, but now folk had more money for the little extras. Some big extras, too, when you thought about it. Maybe that was how it should be.

Woodland Road had been developed in the 1920's when they knew how to build big houses, when they knew how to stain and varnish and polish, and used proper wood like mahogany.

The grocer's shop was not exactly across the road. Townley had to cross Woodland, go down Rolling Farm Avenue about 150 yards before he came to the shop. It was a clean, well-stocked shop, set out like a mini supermarket, pick where you like and pay for it. The owner was at the far end, cutting four ounces of ham for some old dear, and a woman, probably his wife, was at the door, totting up the damage on one of those adding machines they all seemed to have.

The proprietor, resplendent in a pink cotton overall, looked up as he finished cutting the ham, and saw Townley bearing down on him. This will be the police, he thought. About the murder. Mrs. Shuttleworth had told him about it . . . just as much as she knew.

'Good morning. My name is Townley. Superintendent Townley. I am investigating the murder of a woman in Woodland Road, a customer of yours, I believe.'

John Smithson had run this shop for nine years. All his life he had worked behind a counter — well, you could hardly describe it as that now — and he reckoned that through the years, through the thousands and thousands of people he had had to serve, he had met them all. He had learned to form a quick opinion. Some he liked. Some he disliked. This one sounded a pompous, jumped-up know-all, full of self importance, and probably couldn't stand the modern ways of shopping. Definitely the dislike box.

'I had heard about it,' he said to Townley. 'John Smithson's my name, and yes, Doreen Masters was a customer here. Usually came in every day, only missed when she was away on holiday. Nice, pleasant girl. Kept herself to herself, they said. But friendly, you know.'

'Can you remember the last time she was in this shop?' Townley laid emphasis on the word shop as if it were a warehouse he was in, not a shop at all.

Smithson ignored the insinuation. He was right. He didn't like the supermarkets. 'Yes, it's just a week ago. I don't know what else she got, but she bought her usual pint of milk and also asked me to cut her a slice of ham. Said she would grill that for her Sunday dinner.'

Townley cut in. 'What time of day was that?'

'About five o'clock, I should think. It was the last bottle. I'd saved it for her.'

'Didn't she come in here at all on the Sunday?' Townley inquired, leaning forward, almost pressuring Smithson, as if the answer supplied the final clue to a puzzle he had been trying to solve for six months. Smithson did not like the man's intensity any more than his pompousness.

'No, that was the strange thing. I only open till noon on a Sunday, and you could bet your last penny that's the time she'd come bursting in here for her bottle of milk. I always saved it for her.'

'Why didn't she take it on Saturday?' asked Townley. 'Save herself the bother on Sunday.'

'There are some people, Superintendent, a lot of people, who like to drink Sunday's milk on Sunday, not Saturday's. Miss Masters was one of them. Anyway, I always kept it for her. Now and again she'd be a few minutes late, and she'd come round the back for it. I asked her on the Saturday if she was doing anything special that weekend. No, she said. Wash her hair and bath that night, and she was going to spend Sunday just lazing about. And her last words as she went out were: 'Keep me a bottle tomorrow, Smithy.' I did, too, but she never came for it.'

'Perhaps she slept in,' suggested Townley.

'Maybe so. She often did. But it never before stopped her coming for her pinta. You're not asking me, I know, but perhaps it was much more simple. Perhaps she COULDN'T come for her milk!'

3

Superintendent Townley paused on the pavement outside Smithson's shop. If all he had been told so far was correct, the time of death was certainly getting narrowed down. He stood, his left arm across his stomach, his right elbow resting in his left hand, his chin on his right hand, staring into space up the avenue towards Woodland Road and Latrigg House, the scene of the murder.

The woman must have been murdered some time between the Sunday paper being delivered and the priest dropping in his letter. Roughly speaking, this must have been something between say 7.30 a.m. and noon. That reminded him again. He must find out what time the Sunday Chronicle had been delivered. And who by. Newman would find out when Father Johnston dropped in his little letter, and the time of death might even be narrowed down to a couple of hours. Certainly the post mortem would get no nearer, not after the woman had been dead getting up for a week.

Townley was still standing in his favourite thinking position, like a huge Epstein model, gazing out to some unseen spot a million miles away, when a middle-aged woman, well-dressed, and looking concerned, approached him.

'Are you lost?' she asked. 'Perhaps I can help.'

Townley quickly came out of his dream. He was always bad tempered when wakened from a sleep, and when his thought-process was interrupted. He looked own at her as she clutched her umbrella and basket. 'No, madam, I am not lost,' he declared. 'I have lived in this town all my life and there isn't a road or back street I don't know.'

With that he set off back up Rolling Farm Avenue towards Woodland Road.

'What a rude man,' thought Mrs. Gertrude Jones.

'Bloody do-gooder,' mumbled Townley to himself as he strolled up the road.

He wasn't going to hurry. He wanted to

leave them plenty of time to get that body out of the room before he returned. He wasn't going in there again until it had been removed. He looked at his watch. Nearly eleven o'clock. Wonder how United would go on today. They'd got to win, got to win just about every match now if they weren't to be relegated. They were at home next week to Wolves. He enjoyed watching the Wolves, perhaps he'd be able to go.

But there was work to do first, people to see, people to suffer, questions to ask, answers to sift. Five flat occupants to see, that was the prime job, with Mrs. Shuttleworth at the head of the list.

4

Gladys Victoria Shuttleworth was born the day Queen Victoria died. Her parents had argued just about a full week on whether her middle name should be Victoria, for the Queen who had just departed, or Alexandra, for the Queen taking over office. At one stage it looked as if the Gladys part might be dropped altogether, and the baby be christened Victoria Alexandra Shuttleworth, but Grandma Wilkinson — her mother's mother — had had a word or two to say about that. 'That is taking ostentation a little too far,' she said. 'One or the other' she said. 'And I prefer Victoria' she said. She would, of course, because by a remarkable coincidence she had been born the day Victoria had been crowned Queen of the United Kingdom of Great Britain and Ireland, June 28, 1838.

Gladys Victoria was born in Bradford in Yorkshire. She never married. Never wanted to, she always said. That might have been true. But another contributory fact was that she was never asked. She was an only child, and when her parents died she lost contact with what bit of family remained, the odd cousin who thought Gladys rather eccentric and decided she was best left alone.

She had been a teacher all her working life and a vacancy as a deputy head at a Primary School in Rosedale had brought her to the town many moons ago. Now she was into her 70's, still an eccentric, a character in her own right. Mr. Smithson had his own little phrase, his own description, whenever she appeared. 'Here's old oddball,' he would say. And old oddball would spend 20 minutes in his shop, carefully scrutinising nearly every item, pricing half of them, before leaving with one small can of Heinz baked beans, for her supper, and a tin of soup.

She had been a teacher 40 years, yet freely admitted that she disliked teaching. A dislike that almost amounted to a hatred. But it was a job, and she stuck to it, counting the days to her retirement in the last few years of work.

But the bitterness which seemed to have soaked into every tissue of her body while she was a teacher left her the day she retired. Like the soul that leaves the body on death, the harshness left her heart the day she left school. Long before she retired she had decided to spend the rest of her life in Rosedale. She liked the people and the town, the countryside was near, and whatever friends she had made and kept were here. But she did decide to move home, and when she heard of the flat to rent at Latrigg House she had gone round to Woodland Road right away, money in her hand for the first few weeks' rent.

And she had grown to like the place, almost love it. It was quiet and in a select part of the town, which she wasn't afraid to admit appealed to her. None of the other flat occupants was rowdy and it was very rare you heard a sound out of them. She had particularly liked that poor Miss Masters, as pleasant a girl as you would wish to find. Although she was a bit too flighty for her liking. And the latest man she'd had had seemed a good deal too old for her, she thought. At least, from what little she had seen of him. The police will want to know about that, too.

She'd hardly been able to contain herself when that delightful police sergeant had called to tell her about poor Miss Masters and ask if she'd seen anybody around the house last Sunday morning.

And hadn't his face lit up when she'd told him about the priest, too. There was a juicy bit of information and tell the truth, he was the only person she'd seen in the house that morning. All day, come to that. Well, the only non-resident anyway. And the Sergeant had asked would she stay in, because the Superintendent would be calling to ask her some questions. But she couldn't. She had to tell somebody. So she'd dashed off to Smithson's before the Superintendent arrived. Superintendent Townley no less. She didn't mention it, but she knew a good deal about Mr. Townley, a good deal that Mr. Townley wouldn't want anybody to know about. And she was looking forward to seeing the said Mr. Townley . . . again.

And he'd want to know the last time she'd seen the deceased. That was the expression, wasn't it? Let's see, that was very easy. It was . . .

There was a knock on the door. A firm, commanding knock. The sort that wasn't asking if there was anybody home, but demanding that the door is opened. That instant. Gladys got out of her easy chair quickly and set off for the door. She was almost there when she turned back, snatched up her hair brush from the mantelpiece, quickly got in front of the mirror, and tidied up the few wisps of wavering hair. The knock came again, louder, more demanding. If she left it much longer, one huff and a puff and her door might come crashing down. But she had to look tidy and respectable.

She opened the door and quickly took in the huge man, raincoated, his hair as immaculate as her own, his fist ready to batter again. I wonder if he gave his hair a quick brush, too, she thought.

'I thought there was nobody in,' he said, pointedly and accusingly as if she had been standing at the other side of the door all the time, deliberately annoying him. He lowered his fist.

Gladys looked up. She knew who it was. But she wasn't going to let on. 'But there was, wasn't there?' she said, as if talking to a seven-year-old. 'And who might you be?' she asked, the schoolmistress again, determined not to be ruled.

Townley bridled. Quite a few things annoyed him and attacked his ulcer from time to time. The misuse of the English language was one of them. The stupid woman didn't want to know who he might be; obviously she wanted to know who he was. And suddenly, although he towered over this woman by a good fifteen inches and several stones, he felt like Alice when first confronted by the Queen. 'Who is this' said the Queen severely. 'My name is Alice, so please your Majesty,' said Alice very politely. Well, his name wasn't Alice. Nor nothing like it.

'I MIGHT be the Queen of Sheba,' he said with great emphasis. 'But I'm not.

I'm the police. Superintendent Townley, investigating the death in this house last Sunday of one of your neighbours, Miss Doreen Masters.'

Gladys could hardly control the smirk that was starting to twitch at the corners of her mouth. What an overbearing man . . . no, still a child. He wanted taking down a peg or two.

'You'd better come in . . . Police Superintendent Townley,' she said, resisting the strong impulse to add . . . 'investigating the death in this house last Sunday of one of my neighbours, Miss Doreen Masters.'

Townley walked in, and without invitation, sat in the chair that Gladys had been occupying up to his arrival. The chair Gladys always sat in. Well, of all the infernal cheek. It was time to attack.

'Robert Townley isn't it?'

'That's right.'

'Late of Greengate Junior School?'

'How do you know that?'

'My, my, Robert Townley, you do flatter me. You've forgotten me, haven't you?'

She watched the realisation spread all over him. It started at his face, which went red from the chin up, a small boy again, caught smoking in the lavatories. Then it moved down, attacking the rest of his body and forcing him to his feet. For once, he was caught off balance, with his trousers down so to speak.

'MISS Shuttleworth. That's amazing.'

Gladys had got him. She wasn't going to let go. Just tweak his ear a bit. Let him know that even after, how many was it, 40, 45 years, the teacher-child relationship could still force its way through the Superintendent-witness connection. Well, just for a little while anyway.

'You know, I suppose if all the children that had passed through my hands walked in this door now, I'd remember them all primarily through one little incident. Something they'd probably forgotten, something I remembered them by. And do you know what I remember about you, Superintendent?'

She didn't wait for a reply. Little Bobby had not yet gathered his thoughts and position. 'It was that day I caught you in the stockroom at playtime. You and Mildred White, remember? Your pants were unfastened at the front, her blue knickers were down round her ankles. I remember I said: 'So this is what you get up to at playtime, you two'.'

Gladys was a little ashamed of herself. She was enjoying this. This grown man, now a pillar of society, probably a rock of respectability, was standing, stooping in front of her, squirming with embarrassment, just as he had done all those years ago.

But it didn't take Superintendent Townley long to recapture the years he had suddenly lost in a few seconds. 'Yes, yes,' he said gruffly. 'A lot of water gone under the bridges since then, Miss Shuttleworth.'

Wait till he got hold of Newman. MISSUS Shuttleworth, he had said. He remembered distinctly. 'MRS. Shuttleworth.' Only a little thing, but if he had got it right, if he had got his facts right, it would probably have triggered something off in his brain. Put him on his guard. Let him get the first punch in. What a state of affairs.

'Can't say I remember that incident,'

he went on, regaining composure as the blood drained from his face. 'Probably somebody else. A mistake.'

'You could be right, I suppose,' said Miss Shuttleworth, a glint in her eye. 'That's right, I remember now. Ada Bridges wasn't it, not Mildred White at all.'

Townley decided to get on before she recalled that other incident at the swimming baths.

'Miss Shuttleworth, my Sergeant tells me that last Sunday you saw the priest, Father Johnston, come into this house, and go up the stairs.'

Gladys, too, had had enough. He was in his place. 'Yes, I've been working out the time, and as near as I can get, I'd say it was about twenty minutes to noon. But I don't know which flat he went to. I only saw him heading up the stairs, and I really can't say which one he went to.'

'Did you see him leave?'

'No I didn't' she said.

Experience told Townley that Miss Shuttleworth had a jolly good idea where Father Johnston had gone, and if he read the woman correctly, she probably left her door open a while waiting to see if he came down straight away.

'Was he in the habit of calling here?' he asked.

'He called on me from time to time,' she said. 'And also on Miss Masters, often around that time on a Sunday.'

'Did she go to church?'

'Not that I know of.'

'Then why did he call so often?'

'I don't know. To convert her?'

'Miss Shuttleworth, this is important. Can you say if any time elapsed at all when he certainly did NOT return back down the stairs and out of the house?'

Gladys thought quickly. She had waited at the door a few minutes, about ten, to see if Father Johnston would return. With Townley still standing, she decided to resume her easy chair. She sat down. 'Well now you mention it, I did leave the door open a few minutes, just to let the steam out you know. I'd say 10 to 15 minutes . . . and he didn't come back in that time.'

Mmmm. 'When did you last see Miss

Masters alive, Miss Shuttleworth? Can you remember?'

'Oh yes very well. She came to my door about half past nine that Saturday night and asked if I had enough milk for a couple of drinks for her.'

'But she had bought a full bottle from the grocer's,' said Townley.

'That's right. And she used it all in a rice pudding for her Sunday dinner. Just poured the lot in and forgot about saving any for a drink. So she asked me for some. I had plenty, so I poured her a little into an empty milk bottle I had.'

'When you say Sunday dinner, Miss Shuttleworth, do you mean dinner in the evening, or lunch?'

'All my life, Superintendent, dinner time to me has meant what dinner time means in the North, the midday meal. And the one you have in the evening is tea. Isn't that what you were brought up to?'

Townley felt himself flushing and squirming again. In the circles in which he moved now, dinner was eaten in the evening, lunch at midday. Whatever the chip shops said about being open dinner and tea.

'There are some people, you know, Miss Shuttleworth, who have dinner in the evening,' he said, hesitantly.

'Then when do they have tea, pray tell me,' she went on.

Townley felt himself losing his grip again. He'd finish this interrogation quickly and resume it again later. In any case he was beginning to wonder who was asking the bloody questions.

'How was she dressed?' he asked.

'Oh, nightdress and dressing gown,' said Miss Shuttleworth. 'Said she was having an early night.'

Townley considered that. It seemed obvious now that Miss Masters had not been out Saturday night and did not intend leaving the flat again until she went for her milk at Sunday lunchtime. All right, dinner time, bugger it.

'But I don't know so much,' said Miss Shuttleworth, looking up at the man mountain in front of her, waiting for that sharp turn of anticipation.

'What do you mean?'

'It couldn't have been an hour later when I heard the door close and then footsteps going up the stairs.'

'But that could have been somebody from one of the other flats couldn't it?'

'It could,' she said, lingering on the phrase. 'But about quarter past eleven I heard the door close again, ever so quietly. And when I looked out of the window, I saw this man hurrying away down the drive . . . '

5

Townley looked hard at the woman who was once, long, long ago, his teacher. For a year she had been responsible for his education, she was responsible in some little way for moulding him into the man he had become. He didn't think he had seen her since his schooldays, yet the relationship that existed then seemed to be dominating this interview now. She was a Nosey Old Parker, and he wished he could tell her so. Instead he decided to sit down, and think a little.

There was a stand chair, hard and uninviting, by the window. 'Always have one of them in your room,' his grand-father had once advised him. 'And if somebody comes you don't like, sit 'em on it. They'll soon go.'

Townley sat there so he could gaze out of the window a moment and gather his thoughts. He sat down carefully and took a packet of cigarettes from his pocket.

'No Superintendent, I don't mind one little bit if you smoke,' said Miss Shuttleworth with a smile. Dear me, what a rude, thoughtless man he had become. Townley didn't hear her. He took out a cigarette, lit it, looked out of the window and consumed the latest bit of tittle-tattle.

Was this woman just imagining things, he wondered. A priest arriving around the time of the murder, some fellow or other the night before. In any case, he didn't yet have any evidence that the Saturday night visitor had even gone to Doreen Masters' room. And she couldn't be certain that the man she saw leaving was even the same man. But if the man had gone to her room and left an hour later it didn't really mean so much since the girl had been killed some time on the Sunday morning. Still, he would have to pursue it, and if such a man existed, he would have to be found.

While he had been thinking, Miss Shuttleworth had found him an ash tray. She didn't approve of smoking, especially in her own room. You couldn't get rid of the smell, she found, at least until the following day. Sometimes the day after that. It seemed to penetrate every corner of every room in the flat and she disliked it immensely. But she hadn't the heart to flatten the man any more.

'Did you know this man?' he asked her.

'No,' she replied. 'She's had one or two boy friends while she's been here, usually men older than herself. But recently there's only one been coming around, always of an evening. I don't remember having seen him during the day. Come to think of it, it was usually around that time when he came, about half past ten, you know.'

'Was the man on that Saturday night the same one who's been seeing her?'

'I couldn't say,' she said. 'I didn't see him going up and then I only saw his back in a little bit of lamplight as he was leaving. I couldn't be sure, but I thought it was the same man.'

'Would you recognise the man who had been calling here recently if you saw him again?' asked Townley.

'I think so. I've never had a real close look at him, him being an evening visitor.

I've caught a glimpse of him here and there, you know, a sort of general look without any details if you know what I mean. I've never seen him before, but then I don't get around town as much as I used to.'

Townley considered. This man on the Saturday night might easily have been calling on somebody else in the house. He'd have to find that out.

'Let's for a moment assume that the man who had been calling on Miss Masters recently and the man on the Saturday night were the same?' Townley went on. 'Can you describe him at all?'

'Not really,' she said. 'From what bit I'd seen I'd say in his forties, maybe even fifties. Not very tall . . . mmmm, what else. Oh yes, he smoked something like cigars, a smell all of their own. A smell that seemed to hang around for ages. Sometimes I didn't even see him. Didn't need to. Just smelled him.'

Townley was feeling a bit more comfortable now Miss Shuttleworth was no longer raking up his years as a boy. Why did so many older folk do that anyway? 'My my, how you've grown. Last time I saw you, you were just this high.'

Years of experience had taught Townley that old spinsters with little better to do often made extremely good busy-bodies. They listened and watched, and noticed things that nobody else saw. And they usually knew everybody's business.

He stretched his legs in front of him. His backside was getting sore on the hard seat of the chair and he would have liked something softer on which to rest his back. All right, so she lived on her own, but surely she had guests now and then. Surely she didn't make them sit on this thing. Why the hell didn't she get another arm chair?

'Who else is there in this house?' he demanded. It gave Miss Shuttleworth considerable pleasure to watch the Superintendent move around uncomfortably on the stand chair. It put him at a slight disadvantage. She liked that. Oneupmanship they called it. Fancy her having one up on a Police Superintendent. Lovely.

'Well, the other downstairs flat across the hall is occupied by Mr. and Mrs.

Rogers. He owns the place. She owns him. Upstairs, well, Miss Masters had one, and across from her is Mr. Hart.'

'The window cleaner?' said Townley.

'Oh dear me no,' said Miss Shuttleworth. 'He works in a bank you know.'

Miss Shuttleworth belonged to the age when working at a bank was the height of respectability. It went with crumpets and voting Conservative.

'I was told he cleaned the windows,' said Townley, his voice rising in annoyance at being caught out on a question of fact. That was another thing he'd collar Newman for. Wait till he got his hands on him, he'd tell him what facts were all about.

'He does, but only this house. I don't think Mr. Rogers pays him. Just does it for a favour I think,' she said.

'How often are yours done? Once a year?' said Townley, sniggering inside himself.

'Every month,' replied Miss Shuttleworth indignantly.

Townley started to giggle. The anger over Newman had quickly subsided as the humour of the window-cleaning stole over him. He began to shake on the chair, an uncontrollable giggle.

'You were giggling like that when I caught you with Mildred White,' said Miss Shuttleworth.

Townley shut up immediately. He stubbed out his cigarette in the fancy ash tray, a present from Bognor Regis, and quickly returned to the attack.

'And what about the top floor? Who lives up there?'

'Another single woman, Rosalind, she's called. There's a film star called Rosalind something or other isn't there? What is it now, Rosalind . . . no, can't think of it. Do you know it?'

Townley closed his eyes, slowly opened them again and peeked at his watch. It was quarter past eleven, he was getting hungry, and he was fed up to the back teeth of this woman. But what could he do? 'No' he said quietly, almost with resignation. 'No, can't say I know of any film star called Rosalind. What's *this* Rosalind called?'

'Come to think of it, I've forgotten that

as well. But it's not the same as the film star. That would be too much of a coincidence wouldn't it? She's a good bit older than Miss Masters. Well in her thirties I'd say. She's a teacher. Takes French at the Comprehensive.

'And then there's Mr. and Mrs. Jones. Don't think they see eye to eye, tell the truth.'

'What makes you say that?'

'Always rowing, and they don't seem to bother who hears them. Coming in, going out, I often hear them slanging at one another in the hall.'

'Do you remember seeing any of them last Sunday?' asked Townley.

'Hard to say,' said Miss Shuttleworth. 'Mr. Rogers definitely, that I do know.'

'How's that?'

'Not out,' said Miss Shuttleworth.

'You what?' said Townley.

'Not out,' repeated Miss Shuttleworth. 'It's what they say in cricket.'

'I realise that,' said Townley, a cricket fan with especial leanings towards Lancashire. 'But what has that got to do with Mr. Rogers?'

'Nothing that I know of,' said Miss Shuttleworth, looking at Townley as if it were his fault the conversation had gone wandering away. 'Mr Rogers, I know, spent much of Sunday painting at the front.'

'Painting what?' said Townley.

'How unobservant you are,' scolded Miss Shuttleworth. 'He did the front door and both his and my front windows. Nice lemon paint he used. His wife got it. He hasn't any taste you know. It's all in his mouth.'

'What is?'

'His taste.'

Maybe it's my age, thought Townley. Maybe I'm not up to this sort of interrogation any more. It's for the younger men. I should be at home, my feet up, dinner on the way — he only said lunch in company — and Match of the Day to look forward to.

'How long do you think he was at the front?' Townley asked wearily.

'Well, he was there when I got back from church. He was still there at intervals and the last time I saw him would be in the late afternoon.'

'I see,' said Townley. 'Anybody else?'

'No. He did it all by himself.'

'No, no, no. Did you see anybody else that day?'

Miss Shuttleworth looked into the fire. She was enjoying being a cat. She felt in a playful mood. What a pity the mouse would be able to escape in the end.

In all honesty, she couldn't recall. On the Sunday itself there had been nothing to distinguish it from any other day. Except Mr. Rogers had been painting the front door. Beautiful, that lemon.

'No,' she said. 'People might well have come and gone, but I don't remember. Although I do think that was the day Mr. Hart said he was going fishing with a friend of his.'

That seemed as good a cue as any for Townley. He'd had enough for one day of this chair and that woman. She'd keep for a while. He might let her loose on Newman later.

'I think I'd better go and see Mr. Hart, banker-cum-window cleaner' said Townley. 'But we will be needing you again,' he said as he rose stiffly to his feet, rubbing his aching buttocks with both hands, something else Miss Shuttleworth didn't like.

Miss Shuttleworth stayed where she was, watching Townley cross the floor to the door into the hall. Just as he put his hand on the handle, she addressed him: 'Superintendent?'

He turned. 'What is it?'

'Do you think before you leave you could fetch me a scuttle of coal from the kitchen . . . ?'

6

Discovering Doreen Masters had left George Hart as shaky as a sapling in a hurricane. You're not expecting things like that when you're cleaning windows — although he could recall one or two spicy tit-bits — and he had almost fallen off his ladder. He couldn't get down quickly enough and had, in fact, missed the last four rungs and bruised his hip as he hit the ground.

The scene in that room had looked like a photograph from one of those glossy, sexy, murder magazines. Unreal, unlife-like, as if the producer and leading man would walk into the room from the bedroom. But nobody had. For a while he had frozen, just like the room, and he could have believed he had been standing there an hour before he had gathered his wits, stopped himself falling from the shock, and scampered down the ladder.

Mr. Rogers was the only one in the

house with a telephone, and he wasn't in. So Hart had run and bounced down the road like a hare to call the police. 'Would he go back to the house and wait for them there?' Hart ran back, almost as fast, and was panting like a hound at the end of a hard hunt when he arrived back at the door. He just had time to tell Miss Shuttleworth before the police arrived. A smart, efficient Sergeant had taken down the bare facts and then told him that the Superintendent would be round later and would like to question him in more detail.

He went back to his room across the hall from the body. The police were scuttling about now and suddenly Hart felt light-headed. His energy was draining, he needed a drink. Was it whisky or brandy in a case like this? Or should it be a cup of tea? He couldn't remember, he didn't care, and blow it, if necessary, he'd have all three. He poured himself a large, large whisky — that would cost me about £1 in a pub he thought — and drank half of it at one swallow.

He put his glass on the coffee table at his elbow and stretched his legs out as far as they would go. Doreen Masters dead, stabbed, by the look of all that blood about. It was only the second dead person he had ever seen, the other had been an auntie when he was only nine years old. She had been in her coffin in the front room of her home in Wigan, a front room that had never been so tidy before or after. A last respect to her. The room had been smothered in flowers, the sweet, blending smell had overpowered him and immediately removed any sense of reality.

It had been bad enough in the living room, a mass of black clothes and white faces, some with tears dripping down, some staring at the peeling ceiling, hardly anybody talking or moving. All right, so auntie Ethel had died. But people died every day, all day, and he didn't remember her having been so jolly popular when she was alive. The table was laid out with sandwiches, ham, and cheese and tomato, and some cakes. They were for later. There were two bottles of sherry on the sideboard, too. Funny, he thought. We only have drink at happy times, like Christmas and . . . well, just

Christmas. Fancy having it after somebody died.

He had felt utterly miserable in that room full of staring, sobbing black and white folk and he wanted to get out, so when Uncle Jack asked if he'd like to go in the living room to see Auntie Ethel, he thought he would. But that room was worse than the other. At least there had been life among the weepers. There was no life here, just sweet, sickening death. Uncle Jack lifted him up so he could see Auntie Ethel, lying there in her long white gown, hands together, face soft and unlined and smooth, eyes closed, looking more like the leading part in a wedding than a funeral.

But he hated it. This wasn't the Auntie Ethel he had known, not that he had known her all that well. It was her, he knew it was her, but what had she to do with the woman who had lived. As soon as he was put down, George ran into the living room, with living people, even if they were all sitting and standing around like Zombies. He vowed that day never to look at another dead body. And he hadn't. Till today.

When his father had died when he was still only fourteen, George had refused to see him in his coffin. His mother had begged him to. 'Your last respects, George,' she had sobbed. But George wanted nothing to do with last respects, any respects come to that. His dad was dead. He was sorry, sorrier than he could ever say. But he was going to remember him as he had been, the jolly, lively, cheerful man who had been more of a brother than a father. Not the smooth, waxwork lying in a box.

Uncle Reg, who worked for the Yorkshire Penny, had got George a job in the bank when he left school. His mother had gone back to weaving after the death of his father, and George was soon able to leave home. He had taken this nice flat in Woodland and in exchange for a reduction in rent, he had undertaken to do a few odd jobs around the house, like cleaning the windows, and to keep an eye on things whenever Mr. Rogers went away.

George wasn't extravagant. He couldn't

afford to be, but he enjoyed life, the luxury of doing exactly what he wanted, when he wanted. He had gone out with one or two girls, well women, but he never thought of marriage. He relished his independence and freedom and he didn't want anybody interfering with them. In any case, he had never come across anybody he would have liked to share his life with.

Doreen, poor Doreen, had been a nice girl. He'd fancied her. Not for marriage though, just for bed. And he'd been lucky last Christmas. He'd been pressing her for a while, trying to persuade her to go for a meal with him or for a drink, but she had always refused, always had somewhere else to go, or her hair to wash, or a headache. She wouldn't see him, yet he knew she had boy friends, he'd seen one or two come back to her flat. Lucky blighters.

But he'd been the lucky one last Christmas. Mr. Rogers always invited everybody for a drink one night between Christmas and New Year, and Doreen had been the life of the party, giving them a song — not the sort he thought she'd know — and even standing on her hands with her feet against the wall, and allowing George to pour a gin and tonic into her mouth. He'd spilled most of it. She was wearing a mini skirt, and he hadn't been able to keep his eyes on her mouth and the drink. Those pink and white briefs hadn't done his nerves any good and he knew bloody well he'd be leaving the party at exactly the same time as Miss Doreen Masters.

He did, too, just before midnight. But old Jones on the top floor had made some excuse to leave as well, and all three of them left together. But while he and Doreen had only the first floor to go to, Jonesy had had to keep on going right up to the top and his own flat. Doreen had been a little reluctant about going into George's for a coffee. It was a bit late, still she had time for just a quick one, she said with a glance out of the corner of her eye that set his heart beating faster than it had done for years.

There was no finesse about George. As soon as she was inside he had grabbed her shoulders and pulled her to him, trying to kiss her as she wriggled and tossed her head. He hadn't a lot of feeling for such a situation, but he felt sure she was only toying with him, not really fighting him off. So he let go, said he'd make the coffee and headed for the kitchen. He felt pretty sure he was all right. 'Never mind the coffee, George,' she said. 'Sit down.'

So George sat down, on that lovely arm chair he had bought at the sale the previous summer. And then Doreen started. Slowly she undressed herself in front of him, stealthily, with the art of a dancer, taking her time as she took her cashmere sweater over her head and slid her mini skirt down around her ankles. George didn't move. He didn't want to. He couldn't. He was spellbound, and in any case, he didn't need to do a thing. It was all being done for him, and in the most delightful way. Soon she was down to just those pink and white briefs and still George sat, glued, captivated, sweating. She put her hands on her hips, stood legs apart, thrust her shoulders back, looked at him and said: 'Well, come on George,' and slowly turned to the bedroom.

That, George reckoned, was the best night of his life. He'd never known anything like that. She didn't leave till after two o'clock, and George was an hour and a half late for work the following morning. He'd willingly have missed work for a week for that. But since then, try as he would, and he tried hard with the woman across the corridor, he couldn't get a repeat. He used to go frantic with the frustration of it all at times, but she wouldn't entertain him again. And he knew she'd had a boy friend or two, he'd heard them coming and going, and now and again seen them going down the darkened drive. And there was one he thought looked familiar. But she wouldn't bother with him.

Now she was lying dead, no more than ten yards away. He wondered if they'd get another woman in her place. George felt better after his whisky and short rest and got to his feet and went to the door. He just had to tell somebody. This was the biggest thing that had ever happened to him. Who could he tell? Drat, that Superintendent was coming soon, but he'd still have time to go out. He'd tell Len. Len was a close friend, in fact they'd gone fishing together last Sunday. Len was a linotype operator with the Daily Observer and there might be a bob or two in it for them if he could pass it on to the newspapers.

George had become friendly with Len and his wife, who used his bank. He liked Len, his sort of man. Enjoyed fishing and drinking and when the two of them went out together, the odd pitch here and there for the girls. All good fun, and they'd struck oil a couple of times.

George decided to walk to Len's house. It wasn't much over a mile and why shouldn't he go out? There were plenty of other things for the police to do. He wouldn't be long. He went out, locked his door behind him, and down the stairs. As he went through the door, it shook him to find a constable standing there. He knew there were several in the room, but the Bobby at the door took him completely by surprise. 'Do you live here sir?' the constable asked.

'Yes,' said George. 'I found the body.'

'Has the Sergeant seen you?'

'Oh yes. Must get some fresh air. Shan't be long.'

'Very good sir. I understand.'

George set off at a brisk pace. Saturday morning was quiet and there were very few people about. It was a bus route, but he did want the walk.

It was a pleasant walk, through some of the best property in Rosedale. There were plenty of trees and it was a pretty sight in summer when the gardens were awash with colour. Len was a typical urban man, living here in his semi-detached in Rosedale, but working 12 miles away in Manchester on the national daily newspaper. Most people working in Manchester preferred to live on the south side of the city in Cheshire. Len liked the North, Lancashire. In any case, he told him, property's a bit cheaper and it's easier to get to work.

The front door was open, so George rang the bell and walked straight in. Len's wife, Rhoda, was just coming out of the kitchen.

'There's been a murder, Rhoda,' George blurted out. 'The woman in the flat across from me!'

'Latrigg House?' she said, disbelief written all over her face.

'Yes, I was cleaning her window when I saw her. Blood everywhere. Must have been stabbed. Police are there now.'

'Who was she?'

'Doreen Masters. Worked at Barclays. I don't think you'd know her.'

Rhoda James turned to the open door. 'Len. Len,' she shouted. 'George's here.'

Len thumped his way down stairs. Every step sounded as if he had jumped his way down, one step at a time. He wasn't a big man, but ungainly. Medium height and overweight — all that beer — and he did everything as if he was badly balanced.

He went downstairs as if all the weight was at the front, dragging him heavily, step by step. He went upstairs as if it had all shifted to the back, leaning, looking any second as if he would topple backwards. His job demanded that he worked what are called unsociable hours, working nearly all the time at night, when people were either warmly ensconced in front of fire and telly, or soundly asleep in their beds. But he didn't mind this. He enjoyed working on a morning newspaper, setting the news into type, catching some of the news just after it had arrived. But sometimes it was the most frustrating job alive. For he wouldn't set the whole of a story that was needed in a hurry. He would set just one part, usually one fruity, provocative part from the middle. But he couldn't go round the other operators, looking for the other pieces to see how the story began or how it ended, whether the fellow had gone to prison for two months, or whether a sympathetic jury had decided the girl had been just as much to blame. He had to wait for the paper to come out before he could read the whole story.

'There's been a murder,' his wife screamed at him as he went through the door. 'At George's house.'

'And if you don't stop bellowing at me

like that, there'll be another bloody murder,' he said, his face reddening with anger. 'You're always bloody well shouting. Shut up woman. Who is it?' he said, turning to George.

Before George could tell him, Rhoda continued. 'George found her, stabbed to death. Blood everywhere, stab marks all over her. Police are there now. They'll know who it is. You'll be famous, George. Found the body. You'll have your picture in the paper. 'George Hart, bank clerk, who discovered the body, was not available for comment today. It is believed he attempted the kiss of life on the body for three hours, but without success'.'

With every sentence, Len James's face grew redder and more angry looking. His eyes were wide and staring, his fists clenched when he finally managed to break in. 'For God's sake woman, shut up,' he yelled at her. 'Who found this bloody body, you or George? Now shut up!'

George had seen Len get angry before, twice before when he had had too much to drink. But this was the first time he had experienced his temper with his wife.

'Steady on Len, steady, nothing to get excited about,' he said, his arms outstretched as he tried to bring peace to the situation.

'I'm going next door,' said Rhoda, drawing away from her husband. 'Must tell Rita. A murder,' she said delightedly as she bustled out of the door.

'Stupid bitch,' said Len, spitting the words out. 'You'd get excited if you had to put up with her every bloody day.' He stretched his fingers as the tension gradually left him. He looked out of the window then back at George. 'Now, who is it?'

'That bird in the room opposite me,' said George. 'You remember. That time you came for me and she was just coming out of her flat.'

Len James did remember. How could he forget. She wasn't exactly a beauty. But she had a lovely figure and carried herself well. It wasn't always the beautiful ones who made all the impression. There was more to a woman than looks. Figure, carriage, clothes, confidence, the way she looked at a man. And this woman had looked at him. And if he'd known anything about it, too, she hadn't been wearing a bra under her blouse that day. It was a warm day at the end of last summer and she'd been wearing a mini-skirt and this blouse. Len wasn't a bad-looking fellow, and although a bit overweight, he had character and a way with women.

He had wished at that moment that George Hart had evaporated into thin air. Fishing? He'd thought of a thousand better, more satisfying occupations in those few seconds he had looked at that woman.

'Yes, smart piece,' said Len. 'Do they know who did it?'

'No, they've only just got there,' said George. He recounted the story of his window-cleaning, the naked body on the bed, the blood, how he had nearly fallen, nearly been sick.

'I'll bet it smelled something awful,' said Len.

'It reminded me of a visit to the Chamber of Horrors at Tussauds at

Blackpool when I was little,' said George. 'They probably didn't have bodies on beds full of blood at all, but it seemed like that. Wonder when it happened?'

'Ay, you might be needing an alibi George, old son,' laughed Len, who was looking much more relaxed now. 'Anyway you know where to come if you need one.'

He poked George playfully in the ribs. But George wasn't seeing the funny side. Maybe the Superintendent was there now. Looking for him. He'd think it was fishy if he wasn't in the house. If he'd cleared off somewhere.

'I'd better get back Len. Police Superintendent is coming and he'll want to see me. I'll see you later. Have a drink later on?'

'No, not tonight. But if you want one tomorrow dinner, come about half-past twelve.'

George said he would and went out through the front door just as Rhoda was returning. 'Don't forget to brush your hair before the photographers get there, George,' she called.

'Right, See you Rhoda.' Stupid bitch.

The policeman was still at the door when George got back. He nodded. 'Sir,' he said.

'Superintendent arrived yet?' George ventured.

'I do believe so,' said the policeman.

George went in, up the stairs, and lingered for a while on the landing, looking towards the door and the room where the police were before returning to his own room.

'Believe so,' he thought. He knows jolly well he's here. George took off his jacket, turned on the gas fire, and waited for the Superintendent to arrive. He wasn't as important as he thought. It was well over an hour before Superintendent Robert Townley came to see him.

7

Townley lingered in the hall. He felt spent after his spell with Miss Shuttleworth and he wished he could go home. But not yet. There were people to see — and he wanted to have a look at that flat again. It would be locked and the key was with the constable at the door.

'Any sign of Sergeant Newman?' he asked after getting the key.

'None at all sir. Very quiet.'

Typical policeman's reply. A standard remark you might call it. Very quiet. But that's what death does, brings quiet and solitude with it.

'When he arrives, I'll either be in the dead woman's flat, or the other one on the same floor. Hart, the chap who found the body.'

'Oh yes, sir, saw him come in a while ago.'

'Where'd he been?'

'Don't know sir. Said he needed a

breath of fresh air.'

Townley trudged up the stairs, back to the room that had seen such savagery for just a few seconds and which was as quiet now as the grave itself. Not surprising, seeing it had been something of a tomb for nearly a week. He inserted the yale key, turned, and went in. He switched on the light and was again immediately seized by an attack of nausea at the sight of the blood, and the smell that seemed stronger now than when he had been here more than an hour before. The body would contribute some of the smell, some of the uneaten food might, too.

He went through the living room into the kitchen where his nostrils were attacked by the smell of rotting food, and milk gone sour. He looked round and saw the ham that had been bought at the grocer's just a week ago lying on the small table where Miss Masters had presumably eaten her meals. There, too, was the sour milk, a rice pudding prepared on the Saturday ready to go in the oven on the Sunday. Why hadn't she put them in the fridge, thought Townley. Thoughtless woman.

The smell at least told him something. This woman had intended having her dinner, she had intended going to the grocer's for a bottle of milk, but she'd never made it. There was little doubt now that Doreen Masters had been killed on the Sunday morning.

He looked again at the few possessions in the living room. At the coffee cups, the small cigar, the pile of newspapers, magazine, the bread knife still on the rug. The Sunday Chronicle. Must find what time that was delivered.

Townley went into the bedroom. Reasonably tidy, the bed unmade, so she must have got straight out of bed to answer the door and been killed before she could make it. Although that didn't follow. He'd known people who had gone all day and not made their bed. Height of laziness that, thought Townley. Shows a sloppy mind as well — what does it matter seeing you're getting back into it the same day. Like a child who can't see the point of washing, seeing that you're going to get dirty again.

But the bed apart, the rest of the room

was quite neat. A skirt and sweater hung over the back of a stand chair, pink and white briefs were on the floor. But no brassiere as far as he could see. Modern woman. His wife had gone through that burn-your-bra stage at the height of women's lib recently. Burned the lot she had. Then she took one long look at herself in a mirror, dressed in that yellow and orange cotton monstrosity, and begged him to run her to Broadhead's in the main street before they shut. He had taken as much time as he could to try to make sure they were closed, but she'd made it by two and a half minutes, and bought a new bra. That would have been a giggle if she'd had to go to her Keep Fit Club that night in just a vest. Forty-two inches of vest wobbling around Greengate Junior School's gymnasium.

The thought brightened him up no end. It was time to see the man who found the body.

He battered on the door across the corridor in his usual fashion, and it was opened straight away by a man he took to be in his early forties, reasonably good looking, thinning only a little on top. He had an eager face like a squirrel, bright and inquisitive, and he opened the door wide to let his visitor enter. Too many people in the north still opened the door just far enough to see out, and even if it was knee deep in a rainstorm outside, they wouldn't ask anybody in unless they were close friends or relatives. You could have an Injun's arrow in your back and they'd still keep you at the door.

Townley went in, through the kitchen to the living room. He noticed that all the rooms he had been in so far were designed differently. They'd all got the same, living room, kitchen, bedroom and bathroom, but all arranged in their own individual way. Just like people. Amazing really, what you could do with two eyes, a nose, mouth and two ears — all in the same places, too. Just think what could be achieved, for example, with one eye, two mouths and four ears, especially if the eye were in the middle of the head, covered with hair.

Townley made sure this time he wasn't getting any uncomfortable stand chair.

That arm chair looked lovely in front of the fire, and he was in need of some comfort. As he moved to the chair he looked round at a room, certainly not luxurious, but very pleasant. The man had taste.

So far, not a word had passed between them. He assumed this was George Hart, George Hart assumed this was the Police Superintendent.

'My name is Police Detective Superintendent Townley.'

Hells bells, thought Hart. Match that if you can George. He held out his hand. 'George Hart.'

Townley ignored the hand, looked directly at his nose, and said: 'When did you last see Doreen Masters alive?'

'A week ago today when I cleaned her windows.'

'Clean them every week do you?'

Hart had gone to pull his other easy chair nearer the fire, and had nearly got it to the right position when Townley threw his question. He stopped pulling the chair, and with his backside still pointing at the Superintendent, turned his head round to see him.

'That's right,' he said.

'And Miss Shuttleworth's once a month?'

'Yes.'

'How's that, then? Do first-floor windows get dirty four times as quick as them near the ground?'

Hart was still in the same uncomfortable, almost insulting position. 'No,' he said.

'Do sit down will you?' said Townley. Hart quickly sat down. 'Now tell me why Miss Masters' windows got four times the treatment of the old biddy downstairs.'

Hart thought. Better be man-to-man about it. Surely even a policeman would understand.

'You know how it is sir,' he said. 'She's a — she was — a good-looking piece, nice figure, well worth looking at.'

'Fancied her, did you?' said Townley with a leer.

Hart felt safer. Man-to-man stuff this. 'You bet,' he said.

Townley's face froze. He leaned forward as far as he could without falling off the chair, and barked: ‘And did you get it?’

Hart almost visibly reeled under the change in approach. He’d have to be careful here. Didn’t want the police thinking he was a regular with the woman, a particular friend of hers.

‘No I didn’t,’ he said petulantly. ‘I should be so lucky. She had other boy friends, didn’t want anything to do with me.’

‘So you tried,’ shouted Townley.

Hart cringed back. He was getting frightened, all of a fluster in the face of these searching questions. He decided to brave it out.

‘Sure I did,’ he shouted back, amazed at his own courage. ‘Why shouldn’t I? She’s a good-looking woman. I’m single. I like my share as much as the next man. Sure I tried. Sure I did. But she didn’t want to know me, wouldn’t even have a drink with me.’

‘And you wouldn’t like that, would you?’ Townley bellowed.

‘Who would?’ shouted Hart, who had now got to his feet. He wasn’t being pushed around in his own home by this knowall. What right had he got to make such remarks? 'Go on, tell me, would you? Would you like it if the woman who lived across from you, who you saw every day of your life, kept putting you off with all sorts of excuses. Kept you dangling like a fellow strung up.'

Townley sat back, leaned his head on the back of the chair, and looked up at Hart, standing there belligerently, red in the face with his anger. Townley relaxed, let every piece of his body go loose, and a flicker of a smile crossed his face. Quietly he asked: 'And what did you do about it?'

Hart felt a fool. He'd allowed himself to be led on by this experienced investigator, and now felt like a man playing chess, his king isolated in a corner, his last piece captured, and a queen, bishop, and rook bearing down on him.

He sank back into the chair. 'I did nothing,' he said. 'I didn't kill her. I just found her.' The exchange had drained him of energy for the moment. He could do with a drink again.

'Like a drink sir?' he said as he started to rise again.

Townley was dying for a drink. None of that 'on duty' bull for him. But this wasn't the moment. Hart was floundering and nothing was going to help him now. 'No I do not,' Townley thundered. 'Sit down.'

Hart sat down yet again, a human yo-yo with a bullying policeman pulling the string.

'Now then,' he said. 'What did you do about this woman's persistent refusal to recognise you, to even let you buy her a drink. You don't seem to me the sort of man to take it lying down.'

Hart spread his arms pleadingly. 'Honestly, I did nothing. She was alive the last time I saw her last Saturday afternoon when I cleaned her windows. I didn't see her when I came in and I stayed in all Saturday night. Never went out, never saw her. I watched Match of the Day and then went to bed. I had to get up early the Sunday morning to go fishing.'

'What time did you leave here Sunday morning?' said Townley.

'About eight o'clock. I had to be up Birchill for quarter past. Went with a friend of mine, Len James, up to Hard Booth reservoir. There all day till it went dark and got home around half past eight, nine o'clock. And I never saw Doreen all week.'

'Didn't that strike you as queer?' asked Townley. 'The woman you saw 'every day of your life', yet you go a week without seeing her and without inquiring.'

'She said she was on a week's holiday this week, so I just assumed she'd gone away,' said Hart, who at last felt some strength returning to his body.

This was the first Townley had heard of a holiday. 'When did she tell you that?' he inquired.

'Can't remember,' said Hart. 'Some time the week before, I think.'

'And who's this chap you went fishing with?'

Townley made a note of his name and address. The times of their fishing expedition would have to be verified.

Another thought struck him. Something that hadn't occurred before.

'Mr. Rogers, the owner, he's been out all day today, hasn't he?'

'Yes.'

'We didn't have to break down the door of the flat to get in after you reported seeing the body, Miss Masters' key presumably is inside the flat, Mr. Rogers was away, so who let the police into the flat?'

Hart squirmed under Townley's unremitting stare. He felt himself sinking again.

'I did,' he said. 'I have a duplicate set for all the flats!'

8

By now Townley was sitting up. It might just as well have been a stand chair for all the comfort he was getting out of it. He edged forward and perched on the edge of the seat. Hart could see no escape. He pushed himself back into the chair, trying to get as far away as possible. If it hadn't made him look so soft he would have pulled his legs on to the seat of the chair as well, keeping every part of his body as far from the law as he could manage.

'YOU have a set of duplicate keys. Why? Why do you need a set of keys. To clean the insides of the windows?'

'Oh, no sir.' Hart was going to take every question seriously. No fooling about with this man. 'No, you see, well, I look after the place while Mr. Rogers is away. Not just for the day you understand. But when he goes on holiday, or perhaps takes the odd weekend away, I look after the house for him. Now and again people DO leave their keys inside the flat, or lose them or leave them at work or something, and somebody has to have another set. It was part of the arrangement when I came that I would look after the house in Mr. Rogers' absence, lock up at night, and this sort of thing.'

'Lock up at night,' said Townley in an incredulous tone. 'Don't tell me somebody sits up waiting till everybody's tucked in, and then puts the latch down on the front door?'

'Not exactly,' said Hart. 'It's always been the understanding here that Mr. Rogers locks up at night. We all have our own yale keys for the front door and our flats, but at night Mr. Rogers secures it with another lock, a proper key, you know, the sort you turn.'

'Yes, I do know,' said Townley with a sigh. 'I do know what you mean. And what if some naughty boy isn't home in time. Does he have to stay outside all night?'

'No, no,' said Hart, afraid that Townley was getting hold of the wrong end of the stick altogether. 'Mr. Rogers never goes to bed before midnight, so if anybody expects to be after that — and it's very rare — they tell Mr. Rogers, who doesn't bother locking it that night, but leaves the key in the lock for the late-comer. He doesn't sleep well, Mr. Rogers. He's always the first up as well, around six o'clock, and so he unlocks it.'

'Sounds like a school to me,' growled Townley. 'Lights out by ten and all that nonsense.'

'No, he doesn't bother about the lights,' said Hart. 'No, it's just that he believes in looking after his property. Anybody could come wandering in if he didn't, couldn't they?'

'If you say so. And you have a key for Miss Masters' flat? So you'd be able to get in anytime.'

'I wouldn't do that,' said Hart indignantly, his voice rising with every word. 'Mr. Rogers has put me in a position of trust. I work for a bank you know. I wouldn't do anything like that at all. That's a terrible thing to accuse anybody of.'

'I didn't accuse you of anything,' said

Townley, who was now leaning back in his chair. 'I simply said that you COULD get in at any time.'

'Yes, but you inferred it,' said Hart, whose face was getting red again with his resentment at these veiled accusations.

Townley was at his best in an interview where he ruled, where he used his extra weight and power to squash the other man into the ground. And when the other man was down he was the true professional, never afraid to put the boot in.

He had assumed his relaxed position again, the employer with his worker. 'What did I infer, Mr. Hart?' he asked.

'You made out as if I'd take the law into my own hands, just because she wouldn't go out with me for a drink,' shouted Hart, who had jumped to his feet again. 'As if I couldn't take no for an answer, some ignorant slob bursting into her room, as if I could force her or something.'

Townley had closed his eyes, his head resting on the back of the chair again, his elbows on the arms of his chair, his thumbs and forefingers together, forming a church spire. 'And did you?' said Townley, quietly, without even opening his eyes.

For a few seconds the room was completely quiet. There was no traffic outside and the only sound was the quiet, comfortable hissing of the gasfire. Townley could just have gone to sleep. He was warm and tired, just ready to doze off. Then he heard the sobbing, quiet but insistent sobbing. He opened his eyes. Hart was still standing, but the fight had gone out of him. No, he wasn't standing, he was drooping, his arms and shoulders hanging down as if an invisible rope was holding him up. And the tears were sliding over his cheeks, cascading off his chin, and Townley imagined each one splashing, splashing gently on to the floor.

Hart did not answer. Perhaps he hadn't even heard the question. Townley had another boot that hadn't had a punch yet. 'Hart,' he bawled. 'Were you responsible for the death of Doreen Masters?'

The sobbing stopped immediately. He lifted his head and turned towards

Townley. His eyes were red and swollen and the tears didn't stop, his wet face was puffy, but nothing could disguise the look of hatred and horror on his face. He shook his head slowly from side to side, backwards and forwards as if he were watching a tennis match. But he never said a word.

Townley was ready for another kick when there was a knock at the door. He got out of the chair, brushed past the pitiful figure of Hart, and through the kitchen to open the door. It was Newman. 'About bloody time,' he said by way of a greeting. 'We'll go in there.' He closed the door into Hart's flat, unlocked the door into Doreen Masters' and went in, followed by Newman.

9

'Right' said Townley. 'Before you begin Newman, I have a small matter of fact to put to you. Mrs. Gladys Shuttleworth is NOT MISSUS Gladys Shuttleworth.' Newman waited. This was quick work. The old dear wasn't who she claimed to be. Well, well. 'She wasn't Missus, never has been Missus. She's a Miss. A plain, ordinary, common, unmarried, unwanted, untried, and for all I know, unadulterated MISS.'

Newman was staggered. What was all the fuss about? He had seen two people quickly after getting to the scene of the murder to establish what he could about the deceased and any suspicious circumstances, and what did it matter whether one of them turned out to be a Miss, and not a Missus as he had erroneously gathered. 'Right sir, she's a Miss. I'm very sorry, but I fail to see what all the fuss is about.'

‘The fuss, Newman,’ Townley rambled on, ‘is about facts. Right facts and wrong facts. Facts, realities, Newman, are the life blood of policemen. Get a fact wrong and you can get a wrong killer, a wrong thief. Another wrong is created. Facts, Newman, whether small ones or big ones, are important. They’ve all got to be right, they’ve all got to be checked. I check my facts, Newman. That’s why I’m a Detective Superintendent. You apparently don’t, and that’s why you’re a Sergeant.’

Newman had been insulted before. As a policeman you got used to it, even when it came from another policeman. Townley was an ignorant, arrogant man, and he wouldn’t give him the satisfaction of pulling rank by being insulting in return.

And what was the use of standing up to a hurricane. It would only blow you over. Better to avoid it, let it blow itself out. Newman said nothing. Townley glowered at him, wracking his brain for the other gross misdemeanour that Newman had created. There was something else he was going to haul him over the coals for. What was it, what was it?

Hang it, it would have to wait.

Townley leaned against the wall. 'While I'm thinking about it,' he said. 'I want everything you can see in this room removed. There's some odds and ends in the bedroom, too. Take them to the station, then we can lock this room after, and there's no need for the constable to remain on duty all night. Now, why the hell has it taken so long to see one man?'

The hurricane was nearly over. Newman clasped his hands behind his back, looked down at his shoes, usually bright and shiny, but now rain-spattered, and then up at his superior officer. 'He was not at his home sir, and I had to go down to the church, where Father Johnston had just begun addressing a group of youngsters. 'The role of the Christian in class' I believe his subject was.'

Newman knew this sort of detail riled Superintendent Townley. That was why he threw it in occasionally, to annoy him, get his ulcer going, to get back just a little of what he had had to take. For once Townley didn't rise like a salmon. He stayed against the wall, breathed in deeply, let the air out noisily, farted at the same time, and looked up at Newman.

What an ignorant, ignorant man he is, thought Newman. Full of airs and graces on the surface, but scratch him, and there's a pig underneath, grunting and grovelling. It was times like this when he hated the police force, when he hated a system that put one man above another, gave one man power over another. They were dangerous things, power and position.

'I couldn't break into it, sir,' he said. 'In any case, he only went on 15 or 20 minutes. Quite interesting he was, too.'

Townley looked over at Newman. He took in that haircut again. What a thing. Why didn't he get some proper hair? Look at him, poncing about. His hands behind his back, feet fairly close together, the epitome of smartness even at this hour. He reminded Townley very much of the small boy at school, reciting at the annual concert. His mother and father, brother and sister, auntie and uncle, grandad and grandma, the people next door, across the road, Mr. and Mrs.

Whatsit from the shop, all there, near the front, listening intently, hanging on every word, every golden word, as fresh as running water to their ears.

'He looked genuinely shocked when I told him why I was there,' Newman continued. 'Thought Miss Masters a lovely girl, good-hearted girl, who had strayed a little, and just needed nudging back on the right path.'

'Nudging?' said Townley, deciding he had better show he was giving his undivided attention to his sergeant.

'Yes sir. His choice of word. Nudging back on to the right path.'

'Well, from what I've heard,' offered Townley, 'it would have needed a herd of elephants to drag her back.'

'He said,' went on Newman, 'that the last time he saw her, as far as he could remember, was one tea-time during the week before last, and only then as he was passing the grocer's shop.'

'Did he come to the house last Sunday morning?' asked Townley.

'Yes, he made no mystery of that. Said he'd come to see Miss Masters, thought it would be a little after half-past eleven. He knocked a couple of times on the door, loud enough he thought for her to hear. He came to the conclusion that she either wasn't in or she wasn't bothering to answer the door.'

'So what did he do?'

'Wrote her that letter there and then. Almost repeated for me word for word what was in it.'

'Did he put it through the letterbox there and then?' Townley demanded.

'Yes, he did.'

'And how long does he think he was inside the building?' asked Townley.

'He couldn't say. He thought a bit about the letter, how he was going to word it, then he wrote it. He thought it must have been several minutes, maybe even ten or fifteen,' said Newman. 'Told me he usually came to see her on a Sunday. Thought she was worth saving, worth giving a bit of time to. A good girl at heart was his description.'

'Just wanted nudging,' said Townley sarcastically.

'Quite so sir. She had been to mass

once, then when she missed he'd gone and hunted her out. Spent a lot of time tracing her. The one lost sheep, you know sir.'

'What sheep's that Newman?'

'It was a story Christ told sir, after he had been accused of receiving sinners and eating with them. He asked the Pharisees which of them, having one hundred sheep, wouldn't leave the other 99 if one was lost. Leave the 99 in the wilderness, and find the lost one. And rejoice over finding it, the same sort of joy there'd be in heaven over one sinner that repents.'

'Hallelujah, Newman, Hallelujah. You're in the wrong job. I knew it. I knew it. Come on own up Newman, you're a priest gone straight aren't you?' And Townley giggled.

Wasted, Newman thought. Wasted. Christ would have had a terrible hard time with this man. He might not have bothered going on if he'd come into contact with this man early on.

'Father Johnston holds mass at eight, nine and ten o'clock,' Newman went on. 'It seems at St. Aidan's they like it the earlier the better and there's no call after that. So after the last mass, he decided to call on Miss Masters.'

'Does he see lots of young women, lost sheep who need nudging back onto the path?' asked Townley.

'I did ask him sir if he came across many such women in his parish,' said Newman, who had none of Townley's bluntness, but who knew how to ask the same question in a more subtle, less provocative way.

'And what did he say to that?'

'One or two sir, was his reply.'

'You know Newman, I know very little about our Father Joseph Johnston. But I have a feeling deep down that he might be the sort who, having one hundred sheep, might lose 99 of the buggers and spend all his time looking for them. If you see what I mean?'

Newman saw what he meant, all too well. Although a woman-chasing priest was hard to swallow. 'And he did say he calls on the others as often as possible, too.'

Townley came away from the wall and

crossed to the window. A dog was wandering around the grounds, pausing here and there as the whiff of a delicious smell caught its nostrils.

'If the priest is telling the truth, Newman, it seems certain that this woman was dead when he arrived. If she wasn't, if she just wasn't opening the door, then she would at least have looked at the letter when he'd gone, wouldn't she? And then we wouldn't have found it behind the door still unopened. And if she'd been out when he came, again what is the first thing anybody does when they get home and find a letter behind the door? They pick it up, don't they, even a circular about toothpaste.

'But what if he's lying, eh Newman, what if she did let him in?'

'Do you think he'd have time to murder her sir? A messy murder like that would surely have left blood on him, on his clothes, he'd never have got home without being noticed.'

'What if he'd taken his clothes off first, ready for a rampant half-hour?'

'Takes us back to time sir? All that in

10 or 15 minutes?'

Before Townley had time to take his hypothesis another gory step forward, they were interrupted by a knock on the door. Newman went to open it. Just as he got there, he turned back to Townley. 'Oh, by the way sir. I didn't get the opportunity to ask him when he last had sexual intercourse. Perhaps when *you* see him . . . '

10

It was the constable at the door. 'Sergeant,' he said, acknowledging his presence. Then he looked into the room to Superintendent Townley, who had resumed his leaning position against the wall.

'Mr. Rogers is downstairs, sir. Just got in, and asking what's going on. I said you'd explain. Oh, and Mrs. Rogers is with him — a right pair they look.'

Townley could do without such facetious comments from his constables, but he ignored the remark, ran his hand through his hair, and got away from the wall. 'I'll come down right away. I don't suppose the folk upstairs have got back yet,' he said.

'No sir,' said the constable. 'Apart from Mr. Hart's trip out, and Miss Shuttleworth's visit to the grocer's, Mr. Rogers is the only other person to have come in.'

'Newman, while I'm with this chap

Rogers, go along to the newsagents — it's just round the corner from the grocer's in Rolling Farm Avenue — and see what time the Sunday Chronicle was delivered to Miss Masters.' He looked at his watch. It wasn't a wrist watch. It was more a timepiece that really needed a strap and a waistcoat to do it justice. An hairloom you might say, given him by his grandfather. But Townley couldn't be bothered to get a strap, he couldn't abide waistcoats, so the watch, which he also intended having inscribed with his name and his grandfather's, was housed in his jacket pocket. It was 25 minutes to one. 'And if you see any pies anywhere, get me a couple. Meat, meat and potato, cheese and onion. Anything. And Newman? Don't be a couple of hours.'

Newman followed the constable down the stairs. Townley closed the flat door behind him, made sure it was locked and then went down to the Rogers' flat. The door was open, so Townley walked straight in, through the kitchen to the open door beyond, through which he could just make out the figure of a tall man moving around the room.

Townley pushed open the door into the living room, and beheld Mr. and Mrs. Rogers . . . and a right pair they looked. 'Good God,' thought Townley as the couple came together. 'Long mop and bucket.'

Rogers was tall and erect, taller probably than Townley himself, although the man was so skinny it might just have been illusion. His wife was small and dumpy, at least a foot shorter and as round as a dolly tub, and when they stood side by side it was like a music hall act. When the interview is over, thought Townley, perhaps they'll go out of the door, side by side, hand in hand, waving a stick and a boater.

Townley spent too long looking at them. Rogers took the initiative, moving forward, hand outstretched, confident and firm, and clearly used to taking charge. 'Morning,' he said. 'Name's Rogers. What's been going on here?'

Townley could not ignore this hand. It was pushed into his, and before he realised it his arm was being worked up and down like a water pump.

'Detective Superintendent Townley. The occupant of one of your flats, Miss Doreen Masters, has been murdered. Stabbed to death, last Sunday morning I believe.'

Rogers stepped back two paces, his wife sat down, and Townley had a quick look round the room. A bit of money had been spent on this room, expensive carpet and matching curtains, a dralon velvet suite, a deep red like good wine, odd antiques that Townley would not have liked to price, including a beautiful, silver snuff box.

Rogers had probably been in the Services, a captain or a major or something, although he'd be surprised if he wasn't the sort of man who carried his Services rank into civilian life with him. He couldn't stand that!

'Murder? Here? I can't believe it. It's impossible.'

Townley hated to think the number of times he had heard that. Why did people believe that the nasty parts of life couldn't touch them? Always somebody else.

Always the other fellow. A dirty piece of life, the sort you only read about in books and newspapers, the sort that doesn't really happen to nice, real-life people, cannot possibly happen to me.

Well it has mate, and it's spread all over your carpet, your rug, and your couch. It gets into the walls and the windows, it affects every piece of furniture, every last tack in the carpet, because it's vile, unclean, vicious and stinking. Man stops being man when he kills. He's an animal with a prey.

'When did you last see her alive?' Townley asked.

Rogers was still standing, but it was taking time for him to regain his composure, his officer-like aplomb. He put his hand up to his face, spread his hand, thumb on one side of the temple, two fingers on the other, rubbing them back and forth over his forehead.

'Don't know,' he said. 'Can't think. Just can't think. Said she was on holiday this last week — but in any case you say she's been dead nearly a week. Last Sunday, last Sunday, just can't remember. Might have seen her last Sunday morning. I'm seeing these people all day, every day, just about, going out, coming in, paying rent, all sorts of things. And I just can't remember. Suppose it must have been last Saturday, but I can't think when.'

Mrs. Rogers, whose theatrical swoon into the chair had produced no result from her husband, who was too involved consuming a small matter of murder, or from the Superintendent, who couldn't stand what he often described as 'bloody dramatics best kept for the Arts Club,' spoke for the first time.

'It was last Saturday tea-time, don't you remember, Roger?' she croaked.

He surely wasn't christened Roger, thought Townley. Not Roger Rogers? Never in this world. How stupid could people get, inflicting that on a body for the rest of his life. Roger Rogers. Holy grandfather.

The croak continued: 'She came to pay her rent. Always very particular about keeping up-to-date with it, she is . . . was. Said she was having a quiet weekend. Saturday night with the television, and nothing special on Sunday.'

'At least,' she said, looking knowingly at her husband, 'that's the last time *I* saw her.'

Rogers had just about gathered himself. 'Yes, yes, quite right Carmen my dear' — 'Ye Gods' thought Townley — 'Saturday tea-time. Paid her rent. Quite right, now you mention it. Yes, Superintendent. Saturday . . . tea-time.'

Townley stared at the two of them. It was almost as if Carmen had come to Roger Rogers' rescue. Got him out of a nasty spot. Townley had learned through the years that the best method of interview often was to say nothing. It sometimes forced out the most unexpected remarks. He said nothing, but continued looking at Rogers, who crossed his arms and looked back. Townley thrust his arms into his raincoat pocket and stuck his finger through that dratted hole in the corner. He'd lost money through that hole, only little stuff, but it was still money. When was she going to sew it?

Rogers continued to stare . . . at Townley's nose. He didn't like it. Turned up at the end like a ski run. Not a nice nose at all. Not like Miss Masters' nose, not like hers at all.

Rogers coughed and cleared his throat. Townley's ruse, one of the wrinkles you picked up through years of investigating and interviewing, was producing again. Rogers spoke: 'She'd a nice nose.'

Townley took his finger out of the hole. Was that to be all? He waited a little longer. Rogers scratched the back of his neck, coughed again, and continued: 'Lovely hair, too. Quite a stunning lass, but her nose was her best feature.'

Stuff it, thought Townley. Wait much longer and he'll be on about her cooking. He decided to press on.

'Hart was telling me you gave him a duplicate set of keys for the flat. Is that right?'

'Yes, it was necessary for emergencies. Hart is my second in command, takes charge when I'm away, you see.'

'Does anybody else have keys?' Townley asked.

'No, just Hart and me.'

'He tells me you lock up at night, and

then let them all out again in the morning.'

'Yes, it's habit. Routine right from the day we rented the first flat. It's like this, Superintendent. You see, I don't sleep well. Don't need much sleep. Haven't done since the war, as a matter of fact. And this house is a bit isolated, a bit of a temptation to prowlers. So rather than have the risk of the door being unlocked, I've always undertaken to lock up at night. But if anybody's going to arrive home after midnight, they let me know and I leave the key in the lock for them to turn when they get back.

'I reckon, invariably, I'm last to bed and first up in the morning. So it doesn't inconvenience me. And you've got to protect your property these days, haven't you? You boys will know all about that better than me. It's always worked smoothly. Don't recall ever having slipped up with it.'

'Did you lock up last Saturday night?'

'Yes, I must have done because I remember bringing the key with me off the sideboard here to open the door when

Miss Shuttleworth wanted to go to eight o'clock mass. Can't remember what time I locked the door Saturday night, but it would be about midnight, because I know nobody was out late that night.'

'Is there no other door for people to get in by?' said Townley. 'No back door.'

'Kept permanently locked and barred,' said Rogers. 'I'm the only one with a key — well keys, it's got a double lock, and it isn't often I have to use them.'

'So . . . ' Townley went on slowly, making sure his presumption was correct . . . 'so when somebody is in at night, doors are locked, there's no way OUT, never mind in.'

'Quite correct.'

'I couldn't do with that,' said Townley. 'I'd feel like a prisoner.'

'Well, as I say,' Rogers declared. 'It's always worked smoothly, touch wood,' he said, feeling his forehead.

'So last Sunday morning, that front door was not opened to the outside world until Miss Shuttleworth wanted to leave to attend mass.'

'You've got it, Superintendent.'

'Well, what time are the newspapers . . . ' Townley did not get time to finish his question for he was interrupted by an insistent knocking at the door.

'I'll get it,' said Townley, setting off for the door before Rogers could offer any alternative suggestion.

Townley opened the door, stuck his head out, and after a few seconds returned. 'I've got to go out,' he said. 'Should only be a few minutes. There's been a new development,' he concluded mysteriously. He went back through the kitchen and out into the hall.

Mr. Rogers, still standing, arms folded, and Mrs. Rogers, still sitting, looked at one another. 'Wonder what it is?' said long mop to bucket.

If only they'd known . . . the pies had arrived . . .

11

Townley took a huge bite out of a steak and kidney pie, masticated it for a few seconds like a cow, and with his mouth still full, said to Newman: 'You were quick, weren't you? You CAN get a move on when there's food about.'

Newman, who had been standing on the drive admiring the garden, wishing he had this expanse of lawn at his own home, pretended he couldn't tell a word Townley had said. Children you can tell about talking with their mouths full. Superintendents needed a different approach. Newman turned to Townley, who was sitting on the front doorstep, his back against the frame, one badly-mauled pie in his hand, another still in its paper bag on the step awaiting execution. 'I'm sorry,' he said. 'What did you say, sir? Didn't catch a word.'

Townley, without emptying the first mouthful, took another bite, and spluttered: 'I said you could put a spurt on when there was food about.' Newman continued to stare at Townley, refusing to acknowledge a word. Dumb insolence. Townley looked up at him. 'Forget it,' he said.

Still Newman looked at his superior officer. It didn't look as if he was going to offer anything for the pies . . . again. Newman was used to it. 'While you're there, Newman, just get me a . . . ', but never any offer of money. He could get it back on expenses, but that wasn't the point.

'The newsagents was closed till one o'clock,' he said. 'Nobody about. As soon as I've finished this, I'll get back down there. Should be open then. Quite nice pies these, aren't they?'

'I've tasted worse,' said Townley, grudgingly.

'Getting a bit pricey these days, though,' said Newman. 'Twenty-eight pence those two pies of yours.'

Townley put the remainder of the last pie into his mouth. 'Fancy that,' he said. 'Don't know what the country's coming to.' With that he rose from the doorstep, removed his raincoat for the first time that day, and strode back into the house. He was just about to go back into the Rogers' flat when he heard the door behind him opening.

'Superintendent.' It was Miss Shuttleworth. 'I've just remembered.'

Townley's eyebrows came together in a frown. Remembered? What had the old fool remembered?

'Yes, it's just come back to me. Russell, it was.'

Townley turned, utterly bewildered. 'What?' he grunted. 'What about Russell?'

'Rosalind Russell. I've just remembered. That film star's name.'

Townley snorted, made some inaudible reply which Miss Shuttleworth would not have liked to have heard anyway, and spun round to the Rogers' door.

Roger Rogers, a former captain in the British, then Indian Army, took the cup of tea from his wife. Indian tea, Darjeeling. He would have no other. It reminded him of those days, now long ago, when he had served in His Majesty's Most Illustrious Imperial Army in Bengal. He had first gone there in 1932, and would willingly have served out his life there.

He had become somebody in India, risen to the rank of captain, had been respected, and, he felt, loved. The climate suited him, he enjoyed the way of life, the people, and their rich history. He had thrown himself whole-heartedly into the Indian way of life, and spent every available moment, every spell of leave, learning about India, travelling, seeing the vast, beautiful country for himself.

When the British Government had announced it would transfer power into Indian hands in 1948, he had wept. It was only a matter of time before he was pensioned off, and had to return to England where he took over a small tobacconist's in Rosedale. With the money he had already saved, Rogers was able to sell out and retire before he was sixty. He and his wife had taken over this huge house, split it into flats, and he was now comfortably off, not wealthy, but with a steady income and no worries.

Not until this. Rogers sat down with his cup of tea, just as the Superintendent came back into the living room. Townley threw his raincoat on the back of a stand chair, and sat himself alongside Rogers on the couch.

'Cup of tea, Superintendent,' offered Mrs. Rogers. 'Darjeeling.'

'Don't mind if I do,' said Townley. 'Partial to a bit of good China tea I am.'

He took his cup from Mrs. Rogers. He looked at it. No milk and as weak as water. 'Have you any milk?' he said, handing the cup back to Mrs. Rogers, who was just about to sit down with her own. 'Yes, of course,' she replied. Fancy, she thought. Milk in it. How ignorant. Destroyed the true taste. Like flooding a good glass of gin with tonic water.

She handed the cup back to Townley, got her own, and sat down. Townley took a sip. Ye Gods! He held the cup again. 'Do you think I could have some sugar?'

Mrs. Rogers arose, a numb feeling in her brain, a frozen smile on her face. 'Of course,' she said. She went to the cupboard, took out the sugar, and put a spoonful into Townley's cup. She made to return. 'Two spoonfuls please,' he said.

Mrs. Rogers felt a storm building up inside her. She was a woman with a short temper and while she realised the importance of hanging on to it in this situation, she felt herself blowing up, like a volcano. She turned back again to Townley. 'You wouldn't like whisky in it as well, would you?' she said without a hint of a smile.

'Don't mind if I do,' said Townley promptly. Mrs. Rogers almost dropped the cup. This was the last straw. Her mouth opened wide, but before she could say anything, her husband got up. 'I'll get it dear,' he said. And took the cup from her.

'Been here long?' asked Townley.

Mrs. Rogers ignored him. She couldn't trust herself to speak. In any case, how could you hold a decent conversation with a man who took milk, sugar and whisky in Darjeeling tea? Rogers turned from the drinks cabinet, an ingenious cupboard that had been built into the old fireplace. 'Five years,' he said.

'And how long has Miss Masters been here?'

'I'd say getting up for two years. Didn't live in the town. Came from Blackpool, wanted to start a life on her own, she said. Nice girl, very nice.'

'I did hear she had a few boy friends,' said Townley. 'Brought them back here, too.'

'We don't keep a brothel here, Superintendent. Understand that.' Mrs. Rogers spoke at last. He wasn't getting away with that.

'Did I suggest that?' said Townley, almost apologetically as he took his cup of Darjeeling tea from Mr. Rogers, a proper cup of tea now, with milk, two sugars and a lacing of whisky.

'These flats are home for the people who live here,' said Mr. Rogers, quick to interrupt when he heard the first rumbles inside his wife, and saw the first puff of smoke coming out of the top of her head. He had to take over the conversation. If she bubbled over, Townley might be overwhelmed just like the people of Pompeii.

'There are no restrictions. Provided they don't disturb the others, they treat the place as their home. Obviously some things we could not tolerate. But Miss Masters was a young woman. Bound to have boy friends. And if she chose to bring one or two back that's her concern. Are you suggesting perhaps, that she was a prostitute, Superintendent, and using this house for that purpose?'

'Not at all,' said Townley. 'But if men have been coming here, then clearly I've got to find out who they are. Now Miss Shuttleworth said she thought there'd been one regular recently, and she's sure he was here last Saturday night, the night before Miss Masters was killed.'

'I wouldn't know about that,' said Rogers. 'I think she is right about one particular friend, simply because it was usually around the same time when anybody called, sort of late evening. But I never saw him. As to last Saturday night, just wouldn't know, old man. Took Mrs. Rogers to the bus station after tea. She went to spend the weekend with her sister in Buckland, didn't you, m' dear? I called in for a drink at the Dyers Arms and I don't suppose I was in till after eleven.'

Mrs. Rogers stared hard at her husband. 'You didn't tell me you'd been there,' she said.

'Didn't think there was any need,' he said, defensively.

'But you left me at half past six,' she said. 'And you stayed in that pub till nearly ELEVEN.'

'Nothing wrong with that,' said Rogers. 'Either that or spending the night on my own.'

'You said you were going to sort your stamps out. Said it was a good opportunity. They'd been getting in a bit of a mess lately.'

'Changed my mind,' said Rogers shortly.

Townley was enjoying this. He was something of an expert at it, and he liked to see how other men handled themselves in similar situations. But he reckoned Rogers was a bit behind on points at the moment.

'MEN' shouted Mrs. Rogers. 'Go away for a night, and they debauch themselves.' She jumped up from her chair, spilt her tea, and stormed out into the kitchen.

'Bit hot-tempered Mrs. Rogers,' muttered her husband by way of apology.

Townley giggled. 'Slipped up there, didn't you?' he said. 'Sort your stamps out . . . heh-heh-heh. Bet you couldn't see the things when you got back, eh?'

'There was nothing wrong with me,' said Rogers, haughtily. 'I can take my drink. And I had work to do the following day, anyway.'

'Oh yes, Miss Shuttleworth told me,' said Townley. 'Painted the front door and the two downstairs windows, didn't you?'

'Yes,' said Rogers. 'Lemon. Wife chose it. At least she can't accuse me of not having done that. The evidence is there.'

'Tell me how long you were out at the front,' said Townley. 'It's important.'

Rogers considered. 'I got up about half past six on Sunday morning,' he declared. 'Slept in a bit,' he smiled. 'Usually I'm around six, even earlier. I had breakfast, got the paints and brushes and things together, and I unlocked the door around twenty to eight. I always do, for Miss Shuttleworth, unless somebody else asks to go out earlier.'

'And nobody did last Sunday,' said Townley.

'No.'

'And is there only one key?'

'Yes, I locked up, like I said, Saturday, must have been around midnight, and took the key into the flat with me.'

'So nobody could have got in or out before you opened up at twenty to eight?'

'That's right. And as soon as Miss Shuttleworth left, I started to work on the front door.'

'And how long were you there?'

'Oh, right through to about five o'clock I should think.'

'But you must have gone away at some time.'

'Let's see,' said Rogers. He thought for a moment. 'I got myself a lager out of the fridge in the middle of the morning. Don't know what time that would be. Miss Shuttleworth had come back . . . it was a bit after that. Must have been getting on for ten. But I only went into the kitchen, got the lager and a glass, and came out again.'

'Could anybody have gone in or out

then?' asked Townley.

'No. Usually I leave the door from the hall into the kitchen open. It's always open, and I couldn't have been more than a few seconds. No, I'd have noticed anybody going past. Then I was out there again till Father Johnston came.'

'What time would that be?' said Townley.

'I know what time that was,' replied Rogers. 'As he went upstairs I looked at my watch. Wondered if it was time for lunch, you know. It was about twenty to twelve.'

'Did you go inside then?'

'Yes, just into the kitchen. I'd made myself some sandwiches. I brewed a pot of tea and ate them there.'

'Did you close the door?'

'No, like I say, left it open.'

'So you'd see the priest go past and back out.'

'Heavens no,' said Rogers. 'I was back outside before he came down again.'

'Outside?' exclaimed Townley. 'Well how long do you think he was?'

'At least 20 minutes. I got the time off

the radio at noon, and then I went out again. And it must have been a few minutes more before he re-appeared.'

'You mean to say it could have been getting up for half an hour?' said Townley.

'I should think so, yes,' said Rogers.

'Did he say anything when he arrived?' asked Townley.

'Nothing special. Something about a fine day for painting. Soon be spring. That sort of stuff.'

'Did he say who he was going to see?'

'No. But it was nearly always Miss Masters. Called on her a few times he did. In any case, George Hart wasn't in, and I know for a fact that Mr. and Mrs. Jones are Church of England, like us.'

'When Father Johnston came out, did you notice anything about him? His behaviour, I mean.'

'No. He didn't stop for a word on the way out. Just nodded, and kept going. Perhaps a bit pre-occupied, if that's the right expression. Yes, that was it.'

'Not flustered, or in a panic or anything?'

'No, I'm sure he wasn't,' said Rogers.

Half an hour, thought Townley. Just to write a short note? But he'd maybe been to see the other single woman in the house. What was her name? He'd have to check that out.

'How long did you stay outside then?' asked Townley.

'Let's see. I started on the windows then, had another lager in the afternoon. Finished about five. Yes, that's it.'

'You must have gone in again some time in the afternoon,' said Townley.

'Mmm, for the lager. Went to the lavatory, as well.'

But the afternoon didn't matter, thought Townley. He was sure Miss Masters was dead by then, whether Father Johnston was telling the truth or not. But for the record . . . 'Could somebody have passed here then without you noticing?'

'Doubt it,' said Rogers. 'Wasn't long. Just urinated.'

That's a posh unbringing for you, thought Townley. I urinated. They only say that in court.

'During the day, particularly in the

morning, can you remember who went in and out of the house?'

'Dear me,' said Rogers. 'Miss Shuttleworth, for one. George Hart went out fishing. Came back pretty soon after though. Said he'd forgot his flies.'

'Embarrassing for him,' said Townley. 'When would that be?'

'Well, he went out soon after Miss Shuttleworth. Couldn't have been a few minutes later when he came back.'

'How long was he in?'

'Don't know, can't remember. Seemed a long time just for some flies. I remember feeling a bit surprised when he came down. I'd forgotten all about him. Must have been a good few minutes, I suppose. Maybe 10, or even 15.

'Other people from the flat probably came and went. But when you're seeing them all the time, I mean see them every day, I can't think who was around on Sunday morning. If you were to say Miss Masters passed me on Sunday, I couldn't really argue. They're like a part of the scenery. It's not unusual to see any of them around on a Sunday, so I'd think nothing of it.'

'Well, what about strangers. Or people like Father Johnston?' said Townley.

'That's different,' said Rogers. 'Now I'd notice them, wouldn't I? You wonder to yourself what they're doing here. It's not nosiness, you understand. When somebody like the priest arrives, it just registers. Somebody different.

'Now then. The milkman came, he's pretty early. Came while George was back in the house as I recall. But he only leaves for us and Miss Shuttleworth, you know. Everybody else in the house gets their milk at the shop. They reckon it's easier. They can get what they need that way. But nobody else came. Just the priest. He was the only one to go in.'

'What about the paper boy? You're forgetting him,' said Townley. 'What time did he arrive?'

'Papers,' said Rogers. 'Oh, they get here early with them. And again, there's only us and Miss Shuttleworth have ours delivered on a Sunday. Everybody else collects their own!'

Townley was flabbergasted. 'You mean Doreen Masters doesn't have a paper delivered. She must have got up and gone and collected her own on Sunday morning?'

'Guess so,' said Rogers. 'She usually did. Or asked somebody else to bring her one back!!'

12

Newman sat in his car outside the newsagent's. It was just about one o'clock, but they had not yet re-opened. He settled himself down in the seat a little more and held on to the dying warmth in the car. He looked through the windscreen at the few houses on Rolling Farm Avenue that lay beyond the shops. Very nice, he thought. Select. All different designs, individual, and something in the £20-£25,000 region. He didn't like the second one up on the left, the only one of the bunch that jarred. It looked more like a Fire Station than a home and it wasn't helped by the old-fashioned gas lamp that stood near the front door. Newman liked gas lamps, but this one had been cut down to a height of about six feet and looked incongruous. It was like a midget, with a proper-sized head, but small body.

He did like the one across the road, double-fronted, a bit Georgian looking, with a balcony. But it was out of the range of a police sergeant. Not that Newman was really bothered about money. Not all that much anyway. He enjoyed his work. It had variety, and every day threw up something new and interesting and unexpected.

When he had left school as a 16-year-old ten years ago, Stuart Newman had become a clerk at the timber works down by the canal. He had earned five 'O' levels at school, he had wanted to leave, but had not been sure just what he wanted to do. The job as a junior clerk had been advertised, and his mother had pushed him along for it. Not that Stuart was against it . . . he had to start with something, and it might as well be in a timber-yard office. And for his parents, his mother particularly, any job where you went to work in a suit, was a job worth shouting about. She still lived in an age where £1,000 a year was living in style.

But it hadn't been long before Stuart had realised he was in the wrong sort of work. His mother talked of security and regular income. He talked of boredom, repetition, routine. Today the same as yesterday, yesterday the same as tomorrow, tomorrow like last week, next week, every week. He could not face a life of monotonies. Life offered a great variety of work, and Stuart longed for something that changed every day, a job with a dash of adventure and a taste of the unexpected. On his 18th birthday he opted for the police force.

He had been lucky when he had started on the beat, catching an intruder one night just as he was climbing the wall surrounding Rayden Manor. It was all luck, the right time, the right place, opportunity that comes to some, and leaves others completely alone. Stuart had thought about it after. The man had gone along quietly, no fuss, and P.C. Newman had received a commendation.

'Just luck,' he'd told his dad. 'No lad,' his father replied. 'You make your own luck in this life. Some other copper on that beat might have been holed out somewhere having a cuppa and a bite to eat.'

When an opening had come on C.I.D.,

Newman had applied and been accepted, and his part in the arrest of two men responsible for a series of thefts of large amounts over a short period had given him his promotion. Detective-sergeant Newman felt he was going somewhere. He had confidence in his own ability without, he felt, being cocky about it. The work appealed to him. The hours never bothered him, as it did so many others in the Force. And before he had married Marion only last year he had warned her of his irregular and annoying hours. She had accepted them then and never complained. He only wished he could get the 'Super' off his back. He had been told not to let it bother him. The Superintendent was like that with everybody. He wasn't anything special and he mustn't let the insults upset him too much. Newman tried to ride them, tried to see beyond them, but it wasn't easy. It would be easier if he were ten years older, that much more experienced. But for the time being, the Superintendent's intolerance and ignorance nibbled away at him, occasionally affecting his confidence.

Newman didn't want all his confidence and enjoyment to be drained off. He'd try harder to get above it all.

The blind at the newsagent's shop door shot up, the 'Closed — even for Wilson's Whipped Walnuts' — sign turned round to 'Open for Wilson's Whipped Walnuts,' and Newman got out of the car. What a job, thought Newman. Seven days a week, five or six o'clock starts for morning papers, still there for evening papers, and then just for dessert, Sundays too. Good money in it he was told. It was just a matter of finding the odd five minutes to do something with it.

The newsagent's name was James Cowgill. It was in big letters above the window. Newman approached the man, shirt-sleeved, tieless, still wearing his slippers. 'Are you Mr. Cowgill?'

'The one and only,' the man replied, turning to Newman from the other side of the counter.

'I'm Detective Sergeant Newman and I'm making inquiries into a crime that happened a week ago. I'm hoping you'll be able to help me.'

Cowgill stopped tidying the newspapers into their rightful, orderly piles, and looked up. 'Anything you want, just fire away.'

'Do you deliver newspapers to Latrigg House on Sundays?'

'Yes, just to Mr. Rogers and Miss Shuttleworth.'

'Is that all?' asked Newman.

'Yes,' said Cowgill. 'They are the only ones who have papers delivered that day. They all get them during the week, but the others usually come here for their own on Sundays, although I must say we don't see much of one of the women there, Miss Pertle I think she's called.'

'Mr. Cowgill, can you think back to last Sunday? Did Miss Masters, the other single woman at Latrigg, call for a newspaper?'

'I'm pretty sure not,' said Cowgill without hesitation. 'Just one of those things that sticks. There's four other folk in the house, and it amuses me to see how many of them bother to get up and get down here for a paper. There have been times when one has come and taken back for one or two of the others.'

'Who did come last Sunday?'

'George Hart I specially remember. George came early. Going fishing he was and picked up his Chronicle as usual. Good paper if the fish aren't catching,' said Cowgill with a wink.

'And the only other one to come was old Jonesy. Quite a character that one. Ask my wife. Gives her a good chasing he does if I'm not around to keep an eye on the old dog. He must have been taking back for somebody,' said Cowgill.

'What makes you say that?' said Newman.

'Bought a News of the World and two Chronicles didn't he?' said Cowgill.

'Did he?' said Newman. 'But the two women, Miss Masters and Miss Pertle, weren't here, you're sure of that?'

'Sure as sure. Let's ask the wife just to be certain.' He went to the door in the middle of the wall, opened it and shouted in: 'PEGGY, here a minute'.

Peggy arrived, tea towel in one hand, dinner plate in the other. 'Were either of those two young women from Latrigg in here last Sunday?' said Cowgill.

'No, just the chaps, Jonesy and George. We remarked on it didn't we? Why, what's happened?'

'Yes, what has happened Sergeant?' said Cowgill.

'Miss Masters has been found dead and we'd like to trace her movements that day.' said Newman.

'Dead.' The Cowgills said it together, like a well-rehearsed duet. 'What did she die of?' asked Mrs. Cowgill.

'She was murdered.'

Mr. and Mrs. Cowgill stared at him. Newman pursued the matter. 'Can you tell me what time you were open to on the Sunday?' he asked.

Cowgill opened his mouth slowly, like a film run at quarter speed. 'Murdered! Zoweeeee. That's . . . that's . . . what did you say?'

'I said what time did you close last Sunday?'

'We open seven thirty, close eleven thirty — sharp. Every Sunday.'

'And if Miss Masters, or Miss Pertle

come to that, didn't come here, where would they go?'

'Doreen — Miss Masters — only came here as far as I know. The other one I'm not so sure. Although it's a fair way to the next newsagent's. Right down Manchester Road, near the Black Bull.'

'Right, thank you Mr. Cowgill. By the way, what papers do Mr. Rogers and Miss Shuttleworth take?'

'Mr. Rogers always has the Chronicle and one of the 'qualities', the Sunday Times, Miss Shuttleworth has the Observer.'

'Thanks again.' Newman went out of the shop, quite pleased with his information. Something to tell Townley to make him think again. It looked now as if whoever had called on Miss Masters, whoever had killed her, had taken the Sunday Chronicle in with him. Or her.

13

The day was brightening after its glomy start. The rain of the morning had given way to the pleasant feel of a soft, early Spring day. The blossom looked fit to burst and two children skipped down Woodland Road, clutching the Pussy Willow they had taken from the river bank. Clouds blew fitfully across the sky, and as Newman drove his Ford Escort into the drive of Latrigg House, a robin that had been hopping around the entrance to the house, flew off clutching a piece of moss for its nest in the hole in the surrounding stone wall.

Newman went past the constable and through the front door just as Townley was leaving the Rogers' flat, his raincoat clutched in his hand, a cigarette dangling from his mouth. Newman, alert and eager to convey his latest piece of information opened his mouth; 'The newspaper,' he said.

'I know' said Townley. 'The shop didn't deliver to Doreen Masters' flat.'

Newman felt deflated. A balloon gone pop. Townley might just as well have kicked him in the teeth. He could have waited. He could have pretended he didn't know or listened to him and said: 'Yes, Mr. Rogers just mentioned it, this second in fact.' But No. Clever Dick had to show that he didn't really need assistance. A leg man perhaps to fetch pies, but nobody to assist in the investigation of a murder.

'Let's go outside,' Townley mumbled. They walked back out to the drive, the robin fluttered away again, more moss in its beak, displeased at all the activity and interruptions.

'The Joneses are in, but they'll keep a minute or two,' said Townley. 'I'm going to clear my thoughts before I get to them. This case has taken a peculiar turn. Here, let's sit in my car.'

Townley had driven his car round the side of the house, alongside the rhododendron bushes that abounded in this part of the garden. He unlocked the driver's door, slipped in to the seat and forgot all about Newman until the Sergeant knocked on the passenger window to remind him. Townley lifted the catch and Newman got in.

'Let's start all over again,' said Townley, more to himself than to Newman, more thinking aloud than expecting a discussion on the matter.

'Doreen Masters, last seen alive by one Gladys Shuttleworth last Saturday evening, about half past nine. It could have been later though, because Miss Shuttleworth maintains she saw somebody enter and leave the house later. And assumes it was a visitor for the deceased. That's as may be. She was still alive Saturday night.

'Now, sometime Sunday morning, Doreen Masters either gets up and goes out for her Sunday Chronicle, or somebody brings one to her.'

At least Newman could put in some useful information here. 'Miss Masters was not at the newsagent's last Sunday morning, sir. The newsagent, a Mr. Cowgill, and his wife, are quite definite about that. And they are pretty sure she wouldn't have gone anywhere else for her paper. Miss Pertle didn't go Sunday morning either, but George Hart got there early and took a Chronicle, and Mr. Jones went along later, to get a News of the World and TWO Sunday Chronicles.'

Townley turned, his eyebrows raised, his forehead crinkled. 'Did he now?'

Newman went on: 'Mr. Rogers also has a Chronicle delivered, Sunday Times as well, and Miss Shuttleworth gets the Observer.'

Townley cleared his throat and continued. 'Between the arrival of the newspaper and the arrival of the passionate priest, Miss Masters is killed. Could she have been killed before the newspaper was put there?' Townley mused. 'No, it's expecting too much for somebody to return just to put a paper there. This was a murder of passion, of anger. I don't see whoever did it returning later simply to try to throw us. No, that doesn't make sense. Whoever did it would be glad just to get out of the room without having been seen. In any case, only two people, Mr. Rogers and Mr. Hart, could have got back into the room. They were the only ones with keys.

'And if the priest is to be believed, Miss Masters was either dead when he arrived, or she wasn't in. And if she wasn't at home then, she would have removed his letter from the back of the door when she did get home. No, we've got the time of the murder right. Some time Sunday morning, twixt paper and priest.

'Let's assume for a minute she did get up Sunday morning and got her own paper. Why didn't she go to her regular shop? Why go somewhere else? Don't see that. What if somebody called for her? Couldn't have done, Mr. Rogers would have seen them.'

Newman cut in. 'Why would Mr. Rogers have seen them, sir?'

Townley explained: 'Rogers spent the entire morning and afternoon painting the front of the house. Only went inside once in the morning, again for sandwiches just before noon, and then in the afternoon, and while he was in the kitchen the door was open all the time, and he saw exactly who — well, which strangers anyway — went in and out of the house. A nice stroke of luck that, Newman. A man on the door all day, near enough.

'If somebody did call on her Saturday night he might have persuaded her to go out Sunday morning. But if she came back Sunday morning Rogers would have seen any guy with her, if she came back in the afternoon, she'd have collected Father Johnston's letter. In any case she'd got her ham, she'd made a rice pudding, she'd got everything ready for a dinner she never had.'

'When you say dinner sir, do you mean dinner lunch type or dinner in the evening?' said Newman.

Townley looked at the Sergeant with disdain. 'Dinner time in the North, Sergeant Newman, means dinner time. Whatever they do down South, we have dinner at a civilised time up here, and tea of an evening.'

Newman should have felt squashed. But he didn't. Contrary beggar, he thought. Always going on about where he went for dinner last night, don't you know. And which wine they'd had.

Sauterne or mateus. Suddenly he's back to being one of us.

'Where was I?' Townley muttered. 'And if she'd been around Sunday morning I dare say she'd have collected her milk, too. No, I don't believe she went out at all Sunday morning. She stayed in bed as she usually does, and somebody called, probably on the pretext of bringing her the Sunday paper. And it all comes down, Newman, to a very narrow field. Did you see that, eh?'

'Yes sir, I was just going to say it could only have been . . . '

'Yes, yes, I know,' Townley cried. 'The only stranger that went to the house Sunday morning was Father Johnston. So, Newman, it's either him . . . or somebody from the house. A maximum, Newman, of eight people. EIGHT people, Newman, EIGHT. That's all. But which one eh, which one?'

'Who can we eliminate? Mrs. Rogers for one. She was away at her sister's for the weekend. Saturday evening to Sunday evening. It will need to be checked, but I think we can take it as read. I'm inclined to throw out Miss Shuttleworth as well. I don't see her as our vicious killer. There's only one thing she'd have a bread knife in her hand for. Well, two . . . if one of them streakers came past. George Hart came close to being chopped off the list, but he came back to his flat early Sunday morning, after he'd got his paper presumably. Forgotten his flies.'

'That could have been nasty, sir,' chuckled Newman.

'Thank you, Newman. I have cracked that one myself. So there's Hart, who omitted to tell me he'd returned to the house. There's Rogers, this woman Pertle and the Joneses that we know exactly nothing about. And there's the priest. Father Johnston. I'll be wanting to know a lot more about that man before this case is over.'

'You're not suggesting Father Johnston brought the Sunday Chronicle, are you sir?' said Newman.

'Newman, you slay me. You really do. Here we are, investigating a brutal killing. The priest is the only stranger seen here Sunday morning. He doesn't get to see

Miss Masters, oh no, but it takes him half an hour to write a letter. Now I know you think it's downright stupid to think of a priest involved in murder. But I don't. I have more of an open mind, Newman. That's how I've got where I am. And if the man was capable of murder, he was quite capable of bringing a Sunday bloody Chronicle with him, wouldn't you think? Which reminds me. It's time I went and caught up with the Joneses. And found out what Mr. Jones was doing with TWO Sunday Chronicles last week.'

14

'I wonder what's been happening? What do you think?'

Ernest Jones stopped in the middle of taking off his raincoat, the coat off his shoulders, his hands together behind him, looking like a fugitive, a dangerous criminal who has just been caught and handcuffed. His white hair, which he liked to grow outrageously long, had been blown into an untidy mess by the wind, his tie had somehow got pulled out of position, and the knot had got itself into just the right position for hanging, at the end of the jaw bone. Trust his wife to ask a question like that.

''Ow the 'ell would I know,' he shouted through to her in the bedroom. 'What a question,' he muttered to himself. Trust her to ask a question like that. They'd arrived together, seen the policeman together, and when he had asked the constable what had happened had been told: 'The Superintendent will be up to see you directly, sir. He'll explain everything. Mr. and Mrs. Jones isn't it?' They hadn't seen anybody on the way upstairs, they were both in the dark, yet she had to ask him what he thought had been happening at the house. Silly cow.

Jones finished removing his raincoat and jacket and reached for the cardigan he always left hanging near the door. He went to the mirror, combed his hair into a more organised shape, returned the knot to its usual position, and walked into the bedroom where his wife was busy applying powder and lipstick, eye brows and perfume to that hideous face of hers. 'She'd 'ave made a bloody good Red Indian,' he thought to himself. He turned to her, put his hand to his mouth, and did a drawn out Red Indian whoooooop.

Gertrude Jones put her eyebrow pencil on the glass top of the dressing table and looked up at her husband. 'I think that joke's a bit overplayed now, don't you?' she said, like a mother addressing an errant child. 'It wasn't funny the first time.'

'I've 'eard about this Superintendent,' Jones went on. 'Got a wig 'e 'as. Reckon you two 'd make a reight good pair. I don't know why you bother. Look at you. I allus reckons that whatever a woman 'as to put on 'er face can't be to make it look any better — it's just to cover all t' bad bits. And judging by all t' condiments you've got in 'ere and in t' bathroom, I reckon there's not a bit o' your face that suits you.'

Gertrude Jones was renowned for her quick temper. She flared up immediately, picked up the hand mirror from the dressing table, got to her feet and pointed to the bedroom door. 'Get out,' she yelled. 'Go on, if you can't find anything else to say, get out of here.'

But her husband was already on his way. If the face wasn't bad enough, he couldn't stand the conglomeration of smells. It was appalling. Enough to make a chap sick. He went into the kitchen, which, like the bedroom, was at the back of the house, and looked over the moors that stretched out towards Yorkshire. The peace of it all appealed to Jones and it was only on the understanding that he could have this particular flat with its perfect outlook that he had decided to move into the house.

Jones had been born in the neighbouring village of Mirton 52 years before, son of the village blacksmith, an art that unfortunately was dying.

He had become apprenticed to Machen and Howarth, engineers, in Rosedale, and soon after the war had bought a small engineering concern on the edge of town. He wasn't interested in enormous profits and widely expanding business, but had been satisfied to be his own master, employing about 25 men and making a comfortable living.

He left the kitchen window and went into the living-room where his wife was now kneeling in front of the hearth, dusting vigorously at the three specks of dust that had settled while they had been shopping. Easy to see somebody was coming. When she had finished that, she would do the mantelpiece and that bit of Wedgwood she treasured.

'Tell you what,' he said. 'Whatever's

’appened ’ere, I’ll bet Rogers is ’opping mad about it. Lowers the tone, don’t you know. And whatever it is, it won’t ’ave nowt to do wi’ Latrigg. I ’ope it brings ’im down a peg or two.’

‘You do enjoy to see other people suffering, don’t you?’ his wife said as she stood up and turned her attentions to the mantelpiece.

‘Not all people,’ said Jones. ‘But ’e’s such a snob, the old captain or colonel or whatever it was ’e were in the Army. Can’t do wi’ folk like that.’

‘No, but he’d make two of you,’ said his wife as she picked up the Wedgwood with loving care. ‘There’s a man who knows about the refinements of this life, who appreciates the good things the world has to offer. Not a rude, ignorant brute like you.’

‘Oh yes,’ said Jones playfully. ‘Now now now, what’s been going on ’ere. ‘As Rogers been treating you to a few of the refinements of life then, eh? A little scampi moon-i-erre by candlelight, I’ll bet. And I can just see ’im wi’ yon wine list. ‘And what is it to be m’ dear? A little

Graves 66 I think with your scampi, mmmm? And make sure it's chilled, my man.'' Jones chuckled to himself.

His wife shook with approaching rage. 'Well, it's better than your perpetual fish and two at the chip shop. Or as a special treat, potato pie, chips and peas with a bottle of stout. You've the habits of a pig, Ernest Jones.'

'And what's to do wi' fish and chips?' he shouted, his colour and voice rising together. 'It was good enough for my father and it's good enough for us. The trouble wi' you, you painted bloody doll, is you're forever trying to be summat you're not!'

'And you've lived in muck so long, you don't know anything better,' shouted Gertrude, resisting the strong temptation to throw her beloved Wedgwood at her husband. If she could have guaranteed hitting him smack between the eyes, she might have indulged herself. But she knew she'd miss, and he wouldn't stop laughing till the next General Election.

At that precise moment, somebody banged on the door. Mrs. Jones replaced her mantelpiece ornament and set off for the door. She knew HE wouldn't go. He never did. It was as if the door had nothing to do with him at all. Whoever was there, it couldn't possibly be for him. He could do with a butler, that was what he needed, not a wife.

She looked at herself in the mirror, straightened a wayward piece of hair, set a frozen, doll-like grin on her face, and opened the door. The smile faded away immediately. Her mouth became as steely as her eyes and she almost spat the word out at the man facing her. 'You!' she exclaimed. It was the rude man she had tried to help outside Smithson's that morning.

Superintendent Townley's recognition did not come quite so quickly. His mind was still full of priests, Sunday Chronicles and gaping eyes and mouths when the door opened. The face was familiar, that was for sure. But who the hell was she? He seemed to stare at her for the whole afternoon before realisation dawned. It was the woman, the do-gooder who had wanted to help him cross the road this morning. Or some such fate. A good start.

'Detective Superintendent Townley,' he said in his usual abrupt fashion.

'I trust you found your way this morning,' she said.

Townley decided there was no answer to that. He made to enter the flat, but Mrs. Jones didn't move. He could wait. 'And what do you require, Detective Superintendent Townley?'

This was the sort of situation Townley could deal with. If she wanted a slanging match, she could have one.

'I require, madam, to see you and your husband in connection with a murder which has occurred in this house. Now, I can either conduct the interview, here, on the landing, or we can do it inside.'

Mrs. Jones stepped back, taking the door with her, and using it for support. 'Murder,' she croaked. 'Here?'

Townley and Sergeant Newman walked past her and through the door into the living room. Mr. Jones got up. 'Come in, come in,' he said. 'Glad to see you. Now what's been going on?'

'There's been a murder,' said his wife from the door. 'A murder. Here. In this house.'

'Getaway,' said Jones, with as much surprise as if he had just been told that Mr. Rogers had tripped over the front door mat and broken two ribs.

'I'll be blowed. 'Ere, pull a chair up and get yourselves sat down. Well, who's been murdered then?'

'Doreen Masters,' said Townley, who decided he had better introduce himself again, seeing Mrs. Jones was still in a state of stupor. 'I'm investigating the crime, Detective Superintendent Townley. And this is Sergeant Newman.'

Jones' eyes wandered over to Newman, settled on his face, and then he said: 'Doreen? Doreen Masters? Well, I never. That's fantastic. Do you know who did it?'

'Not yet,' said Townley. 'Can you think of anybody who might have killed her?'

'God, no,' said Jones. 'She didn't strike me as t' sort o' woman to make enemies. Not enough to be murdered, anyway.'

'What about you, Mrs. Jones?' said Townley.

Mrs. Jones was sitting near the door, which she had left open. She was recovering slowly. 'Me? Oh no, I've no idea who could have killed the poor girl. How was she killed?'

'She was stabbed, several times,' said Townley. 'In her living-room. Can you think when and where you last saw her?'

Mr. and Mrs. Jones thought. Mrs. Jones stared at the Superintendent, Jones studied the sergeant's face. But to no avail.

'Not a clue,' said Jones. 'No. Can't think. Must 'ave been in th' 'ouse, but I've no idea when. What about you, Gert?'

'No, like my husband. It must be a few days ago. I don't seem to remember having seen her this week, now you come to mention it. Must have been last week.'

'Isn't that unusual?' Townley said.

Mr. Jones answered. 'Not really. You're not looking to see t' other people. It's possible to go days and not see 'em, and you don't realise it till somebody like you mentions it.'

'What about last Saturday?'

Mrs. Jones shook her head slowly from side to side. Said her husband: 'I suppost it could 'ave been then, but I couldn't swear to it. Honestly, I've just no idea.'

'Were you at home last Saturday?'

'Well, we went out for a meal, got back around eleven, I suppose.'

'Did you see anybody at all when you came in?'

'No, not as I recall.'

'Miss Shuttleworth said a man definitely came to the house and left about an hour later, somewhere around quarter past eleven. Does that mean anything?'

'No, we certainly didn't see anybody then, did we Gert?' Gert shook her head again.

'Do you know anything about Miss Masters having a regular boy friend, just one, in recent weeks?'

'Miss Shuttleworth's been telling you that 'as she?' Townley said nothing, so Jones continued: 'She's a bit of a gossip our Gladys. But that's not to say she's allus wrong. She's a Nosey Parker, keeps

’er eyes and ears open, so she could be reight. I’ve seen nowt, but that’s not to say Gladys is wrong.’

‘What about last Sunday?’ said Townley. ‘What did you do last Sunday?’

‘Let’s see,’ said Jones. ‘We allus ’as a bit of a sleep in on a Sunday. Not too late, get up about nine. I went for t’ papers . . . ’

‘What time would that be?’

‘Don’t know for sure. I suppose around ten.’

‘And what papers did you get?’

‘News o’ t’ World, allus get that, and t’ Sunday Chronicle.’

‘How many?’ asked Townley.

‘’Ow many what?’ said Jones.

‘How many Chronicles?’

‘One, o’ course. Never could read two at a time,’ said Jones, laughing, and looking around as if awaiting applause.

‘Chap at the paper shop, he says you got two,’ said Townley.

‘No, ’e’s wrong. One,’ said Jones quickly.

‘He was certain. No doubts, he said. Have you ever got two of the same sort?’

‘Yes, sometimes George ’as asked me to

get a paper for 'im when 'e's seen me going out.'

'But not last Sunday?'

'No, not then . . . Superintendent, 'ow about a good cup o' tea?'

'No, I don't think so, thank you . . . '

'Course you would. We were just going to 'ave one when you came. Go on Gert, let's 'ave a cuppa. We could all do wi' one after that bit o' news.'

'No, not for me,' Townley insisted.

'Go on Gert, take no notice, course they'd love one. You get along and make one for us.'

Townley looked up at the ceiling, and gave up. He'd only just had a drink. He certainly didn't want another. But Jones seemed determined to get his wife out of the room.

Mrs. Jones went into the kitchen, glad to leave her husband who, she felt, was lying up to his back teeth. She couldn't say then, but however many papers he had bought last Sunday, it had taken him an extremely long time to bring them home. She reckoned a walk to the shops and back, unless something special was involved, would take 20 minutes. Her husband had been over three quarters of an hour.

Maybe he had seen somebody and stood talking. He was good at that. And he had said Roger had been painting the front of the house. But it looked as if Miss Masters had been killed around the same time, and her husband was going to have to account for that 25 or 30 minutes' lost time.

Little did she know, but as soon as she had left the room, he had started accounting.

''Ad to get 'er out, so's I could tell you proper,' he blurted out as soon as his wife had closed the door behind her. 'You're reight. I did get two Chronicles last week.'

'And who was the other one for?' demanded Townley, now on the edge of his seat, pushing his ample chin forward, glaring at one of the six people he considered could have committed this crime. 'WHO?'

Jones scratched the back of his neck and got up from his chair. Suddenly he had gone dry. He could make no saliva for his mouth, which felt as dry and dirty and cracked as a water hole in a heat wave. His parched tongue forced its way over bone-dry lips. 'Miss Masters,' he groaned. 'T' paper were for Miss Masters!'

15

Newman and Townley sat up. They hardly moved, but their backs had straightened, their senses sharpened as if they dare not miss a word or a movement. They were on alert.

'Well, well now,' said Townley, trying hard to hide the feeling of triumph that was creeping over him. 'So you got the extra Chronicle for Miss Masters. Last Sunday morning? And what time would you say you got back here?'

'I suppose about twenty past ten, but . . . '

Townley interrupted. 'And who was around at the time?'

'Rogers was painting out front. 'E were there when I went out and when I got back. But you know, I didn't . . . '

'Now then, Mr. Jones,' put in Townley again. 'Step by step, if you please. Did you go straight to Miss Masters' flat as soon as you came in?'

'Yes, but . . . '

'WHY?' Townley shouted as loud as he dared without bringing Mrs. Jones back to interrupt the flow.

'To give 'er t' paper!'

'But WHY did you want to give her a paper? Had she asked you for one?'

'No,' confessed Jones. He looked around to make sure his wife was not reappearing. 'It were just a way to get to talk to 'er, that's all.'

'And why did you want to talk to her?' said Townley through closed teeth.

'Oh 'ell, I fancied t' woman,' said Jones. 'I wanted a bit, and this 'ad worked once before.'

'You'd better tell me about that, Mr. Jones.'

Jones's colour was coming back into his cheeks. He was in a corner, but his confidence was growing. The police were after a murderer anyway weren't they, not an adulterer.

'I knew like anybody else that Doreen 'ad a few boyfriends. She weren't a whore by any means, but she cast 'er favours about a bit, wi' t' wind so to speak. She went t' way t' breeze took 'er and she always seemed to me t' sort o' woman that if you persisted enough you'd get summat sooner or later. Well, I tried once or twice, chatted 'er up a bit like, you know. Brought 'er a paper back a couple o' times, caught 'er on t' stairs, and then I 'it jackpot one day.

'I wasn't going to waste time on t' woman anyway. There's plenty more fish in t' sea, and I don't 'ave to go grovelling after any of 'em. But I brought t' paper back one Sunday morning, got 'er out o' bed I did, and I must 'ave caught 'er in t' reight mood. Invited me in and before you could say Bob's Your Uncle I were on t' job. Proper good she were, too,' said Jones with a leer. 'Knew 'er onions, she did.'

'Is that the only time you caught her right?' asked Townley.

'Ay. She did promise I could 'ave a drink wi' 'er in 'er room at Christmas. That's when Rogers throws a bit of a party for all t' residents, you know. T' wife went to bed pretty early, and I were going to follow Doreen up to 'er room.'

'And what happened?'

'What 'appened? Bloody George nipped in. George 'Art. Ay, I've no complaints though. First there, first served, that's my motto, and may t' best man win. I don't know whether 'e'd 'ad a word or not as well, but 'e beat me to t' draw, the bugger.'

'So you tried again last Sunday?'

'Ay, I did. But she weren't in,' Jones added hastily. 'Leastwise she didn't answer t' door. She could 'ave been dead, couldn't she?' he asked, looking first at Townley, then at Newman, then back to Townley.

'I don't know I'm sure,' said Townley. 'I was hoping you'd tell me.'

''Ere, I didn't kill that girl,' said Jones, starting forward. 'That 'ad nowt to do wi' me. I knocked on t' door, there were no answer, so I went away.'

'Are you sure, Mr. Jones?'

'You bet your life I'm sure, you ask Rosalind Pertle.'

Rosalind, thought Townley. Oh yes, Rosalind Russell.

'Rosalind Pertle,' he repeated. 'And what has she got to do with this?'

Jones looked round again at the kitchen door, then back at Townley. 'Well, wi' Doreen not answering . . . '

'Don't tell me,' said Townley drily. 'No answer from Doreen, so you thought you'd try your luck with Rosalind.'

'That's reight,' said Jones. 'She's a stuck-up one that. Didn't seem to want to know anybody, but I thought I'd give 'er a try.'

'You must have been bursting,' said Townley. 'Was this the first time, last Sunday morning?'

'No,' confessed Jones. 'I'd tried 'er once before, caught 'er coming in one night, pretty late it were. I'd put t' car away, be about quarter past eleven, and she were just coming up t' drive. Chatted 'er up, damn near invited myself in, but she weren't 'aving any.

'She give me one o' them looks, you know. Makes you feel you've crawled out from under a stone. I didn't bother. She's no Raquel Welch and what the 'ell. Plenty o' fish.'

'But you went again Sunday morning?' said Townley.

'Ay, thought I'd chance my arm again. She were in, dressed to kill she were. Told 'er I'd been to t' shop, would she like this paper. I'd got a spare. Looked down 'er nose she did. 'Sunday Chronicle,' she said, all bloody snooty. 'Do you read that rubbish?' she said. 'I wouldn't have it in the house.' So I said: 'Well never mind t' paper then, 'ow about a cup o' tea love?' Tried putting my arm round 'er waist, sort o' friendly like, and she shot back. Well, I couldn't do to mess around. I weren't wasting time on 'er. She weren't worth t' big build-up, you know, fancy meal and wine and candlelight. She were strictly one o' them, do you or don't you. I don't believe in wasting words wi' 'er sort. I'm one o' these straight to t' point. 'Do you take 'em off, or pull 'em to one side, love.' You know.'

Newman winced. Police work brought you into touch with all sorts of people, but it never stopped him feeling appalled at the depths of some folk. Seeing how the other half lives. The art of chatting up a woman. The subtle, refined, charming approach of the man about town . . . 'Do you take 'em off, or pull 'em to one side, love?' What a wonderful pair these two would make, thought Newman. Two animals together. The stallion and the pig. What a sickening thought.

Just at this moment, Mrs. Jones returned to the room, china cups and saucers, sugar, silver spoons, milk, all on the trolley that she pushed in front of the fire. Newman noticed that as she neared her husband, she looked up and glared at him, with almost hatred in her eyes.

Perhaps she had been eavesdropping. Newman could not resist a smile to himself. He'd like to be a fly on the wall later if she had.

'The tea's just brewing,' said Mrs. Jones as she went back into the kitchen.

'Then what happened?' Townley said to Jones.

'Eh?' said Jones. 'Oh, wi' bossy Rossy you mean. Looked at me like I were dirt, said she'd 'ad to deal wi' dirty old men like me before, and if I pestered 'er any more she'd go straight to t' wife.'

'And I'm sure you had some well-chosen words in return?' said Townley.

'Yes, I did,' said Jones. 'I told 'er to piss off and threw t' Chronicle at 'er.'

'Very nice,' said Townley. 'Very nice. Did you see anybody else at all that morning?'

'No, as I say, Rogers were at t' front, painting. And yon old battleaxe were the only other person as I saw.'

'Do you know Father Johnston at all?' said Townley.

'Ay, I do. I'm no catholic, in fact I'm no churchgoer, but I know this fellow. Seen 'im 'ere once or twice, too. Seeing Doreen 'e were. Why do you ask?'

'He was here last Sunday morning. Did you see him?'

'No.'

'What about your wife?'

'Well, if she did, she never said. She didn't go out o' the flat all morning, at least while I were 'ere. Talking o' Father Johnston, I must tell you . . . '

But before Jones could say any more, his wife came back into the room carrying a large flowered tea pot, enveloped in an enormous cosy. 'Strong or weak, Superintendent,' she said as she prepared to pour.

'Strong,' said Townley. 'I was asking your husband if either of you had seen Father Johnston here last Sunday morning.'

'Not me,' said Mrs. Jones. 'I didn't move out of this flat last Sunday morning. I didn't see anybody,' she said, handing a cup to the Superintendent. 'Sergeant?'

'Yes, strong please, Mrs. Jones,' he said.

What a nice, polite man, she thought. Wonder how he stands that boor all day, every day. Still, she thought, I've been putting up with one all my married life. And that's not just through the daytime either . . .

'What about some cake for the gentlemen?' Jones said to his wife.

'No, not for me', said Townley.

'I haven't taken it out of the box yet,' said Mrs. Jones, glowering at her husband, who knew the cake had been bought specially for tea tomorrow when their friends, Jean and George, were visiting.

'Well I want some,' said Jones, uncompromisingly.

Mrs. Jones hesitated a moment, then,

managing to contain her mounting rage, she stormed out of the door, her lips tight together, her eyes ablaze.

'Now then,' said Jones. 'Before she gets back, I must tell you about this 'ere priest. Fantastic this is. About three week ago, I went into Manchester, a club I goes to now and then, strip club, Blue Elephant. 'Ave you 'eard of it?'

'Oh yes,' said Townley. 'Very select.'

'Ay, well,' said Jones. 'Get some good stuff there you know. Reight coloured elephant an' all. Some o' them girls knows what they're doing.'

'And no doubt they DO take them off,' said the Superintendent.

'Ay, you're reight there,' said Jones. 'Not all of 'em though. Anyway, one night they 'ad this big bird on. Reight favourite she is. Must 'ave a fifty-inch bust. Proper lovely. Anyway, she does this strip, brings th' 'ouse down she does. Off she goes and I'm looking round when I see this chap at t' back, dark glasses and all mod gear, flares, platform 'eels, open-neck shirt, bloody necklace, the lot. I thought 'e looked familiar, though I couldn't think of it for t' moment. Then 'e takes his glasses off, and I knew who it were.'

'Don't tell me,' exclaimed Townley. 'I don't believe it.'

'Ay,' said Jones. 'Father bleeding Johnston. Could 'ave knocked me over wi' a feather.'

'Are you sure?' said Townley. 'Absolutely certain. Could you be wrong?'

'No, not me,' Jones replied. 'I knows Father Johnston, and I'm telling you — that were 'im. Proper enjoying 'imself 'e were. He weren't drinking beer though. Looked like Coca Cola to me. Maybe 'e doesn't drink. Still, you don't need a drink at a show like that.' Jones cackled at the thought.

Townley put down his cup of tea, hardly touched, on the trolley near his right arm. 'I think it's time I had a word with Father Johnston,' he said, rising from his chair. 'I'll be wanting to see you again though Mr. Jones. And I'd rather, just for today, if you'd stay in so I can get hold of you right away if need be.' He looked over at Newman, still fondling his cup of tea, hoping the Superintendent would at least let him finish his drink. Townley nodded his head to the door. 'Come on,' he said. 'Work to be done.'

Newman sighed, got up and walked over to the trolley where he replaced his cup. At this moment Mrs. Jones, bearing an exquisite chocolate cake, smothered in cream, came through the kitchen door. 'You're not going,' she said to Townley, her forehead wrinkled in astonishment.

'Yes, duty calls,' he said.

Her mouth opened. 'But what about the cake?'

Townley moved towards her. 'Well now you've cut into it I'll have a piece for the journey if that's all right,' he said and with great difficulty picked up one of the four pieces she had sliced. He bit into it as he went back to the door, the cake flattened, the cream spread, a blob fell on to the floor, more spread itself around Townley's packed mouth. 'Very nice,' he managed to splutter out, spraying Mrs. Jones with chocolate crumbs. 'Must be off.' He opened the door and went through, followed quickly by Newman.

For once Gertrude Jones was lost for

words. Her mouth opened and closed like a fish stranded on the river bank, and her husband thought she was going to explode. He felt he should say something. 'I must say it does look very nice,' he said, nodding towards the cake. His wife, the fury still building up inside her, got hold of the cake in both hands, and squeezed it as if it were the Superintendent's neck. Cream squirted out over her hands and dress, and dropped on to the carpet. Her face went purple in her rage. Thoughtlessly, she wiped her hands down the front of her dress as if it were a pinafore, and at last she screamed out: 'The sod. THE SOD. I'll sue that bloody police force.'

16

Newman closed the door quietly behind him. He knew there would be enough noise inside that room for a few minutes without any need for him to add to it. Townley, his raincoat in one hand, stretched his arms in the air, yawned mightily, and then said to Newman: 'Did you believe him?'

'It sounded convincing enough, sir. Not the sort of thing you make up, is it, throwing the paper in a woman's face?'

'Doesn't prove anything,' said Townley. 'He could still have killed Masters, taken his paper with him, and tried his luck again. Or he could have done it the other way round . . . brush off by Pertle followed by a try with Masters. Anyway, I'm off to see this double-faced priest, and I also want to call on the chap Hart went fishing with. What's his name?' Townley took his notebook out of his jacket pocket . . . 'Len James, 63 Monmouth Avenue. You wait here for this Pertle woman. And you might have another word with Hart. He didn't tell me he came back to collect his flies after he'd picked up his paper last Sunday morning. I'll see you back here when I've finished.'

The two of them set off down the stairs. As they passed the murdered woman's door, Townley lingered. 'I wonder if Rogers got his share here?' he mused. 'If everybody was knocking on the door, and wives knew about it . . . if you get the chance, see if you can't get a word with Mrs. Jones, on her own,' he added, looking back at Newman.

They continued down the stairs and out of the front door where the constable was still standing guard, an immovable sentry. The sun was trying to break through, and after the rain of the morning the glare forced Townley to shield his eyes with his hand.

'Turning out nice now, sir,' said the constable. Townley grunted and headed for his car.

‘Things not going so well, sarge?’ asked P.C. Andrew Connolly, turning his attention to Newman.

‘I wouldn’t say that,’ said Newman. ‘We’ve had one or two pieces of luck with this one. Just a matter of sorting the wheat from the chaff, then maybe we’ll get somewhere.’

‘The goats from the sheep,’ said the constable by way of keeping the conversation going.

Townley’s Rover 2000 roared round the side of the house, down the drive, and with hardly a hint at braking at the gates, out on to Woodland Road.

‘Or the pigs from the bulls,’ muttered Newman.

‘Beg your pardon, sarge?’

‘Oh, nothing Andy. Just thinking out loud.’

Newman went back into the house and the entrance hall. Was it going so well? It must be if Townley was right and the suspects could be narrowed down to a mere six. But who was emerging as the most likely murderer?

Father Johnston? He was certainly head

of the list, and he was having to come round to Townley's view that here, indeed, was a man with opportunity, and, judging from his need to find solace at the strip clubs, a man who could well have had motive.

Ernest Jones? Again, opportunity looked to be there. Was he driven to the point of no return by a woman teasing and frustrating? He said there were plenty more women in his particular ocean, but this was a murder in anger, committed on the spur of the moment, the human kettle that had boiled over.

George Hart? He didn't know enough about him, but apparently the same opportunity and motive. He'd be able to make a better assessment after he had seen him.

Roger Rogers? Only his word for it that he never strayed from the front door.

Mrs. Shuttleworth — blow it, MISS Shuttleworth — and Mrs. Rogers could be discounted, but what about Mrs. Jones. A formidable woman, Newman thought. Not one to let infidelity go on right under her nose, and a woman who looked capable of being roused to the right passion for such a crime.

He looked at his watch. Just after quarter past two. Time for a word with Hart.

17

Townley screeched to a halt at the corner of Billings Road and Ashworth Drive. Blast the lights. Another half second and he would have been through. Townley drove his car as if the roads of Rosedale were one enormous Brands Hatch. He considered himself a good driver, nay brilliant, and speed was only dangerous when allied to lack of concentration and control. He pushed in the automatic cigarette lighter on the dashboard and reached in his pocket for his packet of No. 6. Nothing there. Blast it. He'd forgotten. He'd had the last. He'd stop at the tobacconist's in Martin Road on his way to the priest's.

Townley looked at the lights, not those directly in front, but the ones controlling the road crossing in front of him. As soon as he could see the amber replace the green, he shifted into gear, and as red came up for the other traffic, he let out the clutch and shot away across the road. His own light had not had time to change to green, but what the hell, he was in a hurry.

Two minutes later he stopped to buy himself 20 Player's No. 6 — 'Better make it 40' — before he finished his journey to Father Johnston's home. He left the car on the road, completely blocking the drive to the priest's house, walked up the rhododendron-flanked path, and rang the doorbell. The door opened immediately to its full width, held open by Father Johnston's housekeeper, Miss Bridget Moran.

Bridget Moran had taken care of priests, on and off, one way and another, for nigh on 40 years. She had protected and mollycoddled them and prepared them for the sinful world and unsavoury people with which they were forced to come into contact. Miss Moran herself should have been a nun. But they didn't have the gin and the television in the convents. She would settle for this way of doing her bit for the Madonna.

She liked the North. She had taken to

it the moment she had first seen it back in the 1930's when she had arrived in Liverpool. Not that she thought of Liverpool as being typical of Lancashire. Too many flipping Irish folk there for that, but it had been her first taste of the county — and she had wanted more.

She quickly appraised the man at the door. A huge bulk of a man, reasonably expensive suit and shoes, funny hair, and smoking. Didn't like that.

'Yes,' she said, as she threw the door open wide in her customary welcoming fashion.

'I'm from the police, and I want to see Father Johnston,' he said.

'Well, he's rather busy right now and the police have already been to see him,' said Bridget, putting on her protective hat, ready to take on the world and save her beloved Father from undue interruptions.

'I don't care if the Pope and Jesus Christ are in there with him. I'm Detective Superintendent Townley and if he's in I aim to see him NOW,' said Townley, moving in through the open door and into the spacious, plant-filled hall.

That's one man I shouldn't have opened the door to, thought Bridget. Just a crack and then slammed it in his face. But she knew authority when she smelled it and there was no point in making a fuss. After all, she didn't reckon she could throw this brute out. But she could still protest. 'He is in the middle of preparing his sermon, you know, and did say specifically that he was not to be interrupted. The sermon is one time of the week when he can address the congregation as a whole and it is important that he gives full consideration to his words. Full, unbroken consideration,' she emphasised, her Irish accent growing stronger.

'I am investigating a murder,' said the Superintendent. 'That is more important. And my time is precious, too. Now will you tell him I'm here?'

Bridget Moran scowled at Robert Townley. Robert Townley glowered at Bridget Moran. There was only one winner. 'Wait here please,' said Bridget, going down the long hall and into the study door at the bottom. She was gone only a few seconds, then stuck her head out of the study door and called back down the hall. 'In here please.'

Townley walked down the hall and into a spacious study, set at the corner of the house with windows on two sides. A pleasant room, thought Townley. One wall was entirely taken up with shelves of books, all religious books as far as Townley could see, not a Playboy or a Men Only among them. An oversize Mary and the Child stood on a table in a corner of the room and the priest's desk stood in another corner, between the two windows. Father Johnston got up and walked over to Townley. 'Thank you Bridget,' he said to the woman who was still standing at the door. She left.

Father Johnston was not Townley's idea of a man of Holy Orders. His hair was too long for one thing, he was too young, probably mid 20's, and he was too good looking. He was casually dressed — not in the mod gear that Ernest Jones had seen him in, but sloppy trousers and a sweater. Priests, vicars, ministers, were like policemen, thought Townley. Never off duty — and they should show it in their clothes.

'How can I help you, Superintendent?' said Father Johnston. He flashed an easy smile, more suitable for the stage than the church thought Townley, a confident, self-assured smile, one developed by all clergy for all people. They could never be without that smile. It was part of the trade. Politicians developed it, too, especially when an election was looming. Smile at them all, then nobody can be offended. You've caught them all, then, even Detective Superintendents.

'I'd like to know what takes Roman Catholic priests off to such dens of iniquity as the Blue Elephant,' said Townley. He'd wipe the silly smile off his face, and anyway, the best results were often obtained by immediate attack, allowing no time for the enemy to prepare its defence.

'I beg your pardon, Superintendent,' said the priest, the smile fading from his face with the speed of light.

'I want to know, Father Johnston, what takes you off to the Blue Elephant, a striptease club, in Manchester?'

Father Johnston took his time replying. He slowly went back to his desk, sat down, and stared long and hard at the policeman before he replied.

'Putting to one side for a moment the question of whether I was in the Blue Elephant or not, Superintendent, would you kindly tell me what business it is of yours?'

'Certainly,' said Townley. 'I am investigating a murder, the savage killing of a woman you knew pretty well. And as far as I can determine, you could be the last person to have seen the woman alive. As a man of the cloth I assume the truth when you tell me she did not answer the door when you called last Sunday morning. Then I find that you frequent such places as the Blue Elephant. I think you will agree Father' — Townley lent particular and peculiar emphasis to the word — 'Johnston, that such knowledge undermines your credibility.'

'I see,' said the priest. 'I go to a strip

club, so I am your chief suspect, am I? I must be, I suppose, seeing you have come so hot on the heels of your Sergeant. The Murdering Priest. Oh yes, I see now. Well, I'm afraid I'm going to have to disappoint you, Superintendent. I did not kill Doreen Masters, may her soul rest in peace. There was no answer when I knocked at her door last Sunday morning, and I left a note. Now I am rather busy and I would like to get back to my sermon for tomorrow.' Father Johnston turned his back on Townley as if the audience were over. He should have known better. He probably did know better.

'I am afraid that won't do,' said Townley quietly, moving over to the carver chair that stood at the side of the fireplace, no longer used for fires, but another receptacle for innumerable plants, nearly all trailing, none of them looking as if they ever bore flowers. 'You told my Sergeant, if I remember correctly, that you spent something like 10 or 15 minutes composing your note for Miss Masters?'

Father Johnston looked up at the ceiling. No use looking up there for help, old lad, thought Townley. The priest pushed his chair back and turned it ninety degrees so he could look at Townley. He was not going to push his 'I'm busy' bit. There was no point.

'What I said, Superintendent, was that I was probably in the house ten or fifteen minutes. I was a little while knocking at the door and waiting.'

'Mr. Rogers was outside painting, wasn't he?' said Townley.

'Yes, he was.'

'He says you were in there half an hour.'

'He could have been wrong,' said Father Johnston.

'Not a chance,' said Townley. 'Happened to look at his watch when you went by, and then heard the radio time before you reappeared. Half an hour. What were you doing for half an hour?'

'Assuming that Mr. Rogers is right, Superintendent, I can only suppose it took me longer than I thought to write my note for Miss Masters.'

'Twenty-five minutes?' said Townley.

'I suppose it must have been.'

'A long time don't you think. Just to write thirty or forty words?'

'A priest has to be careful with words, Superintendent,' said Father Johnston. 'Especially written words, to single women.'

'Especially single woman of doubtful repute,' said Townley.

'I didn't say that,' said the priest.

'No, I did,' said Townley. 'How well did you know Miss Masters? Or Doreen, I think you called her in your note.'

'I had known her several months. She came to mass one morning for the first time. I try to make a point of having a word with newcomers, welcoming them, encouraging them to come again. Often some unusual event, tragic often, has forced them to church, and they need help.'

'Did she?' asked Townley.

'Well, she didn't come again, and after a week or two, I made inquiries. Miss Shuttleworth, she's on the ground floor at Latrigg you know, told me about her, so I used to visit her, try to get her to return. But I didn't succeed. She never came back to church. But I persisted. I believe that's what I'm called to do, to make people see the light and follow the Lord.'

'How often did you call on her?' Townley asked.

'I couldn't say. Sunday lunchtime was a convenient time for me, right after the final mass, and usually I knew I would find her at home.'

'Do you tend all your flock with the same . . . er . . . persistence?' Townley asked, searching hard for the right word.

'People are different, Superintendent,' said the priest. 'I'm sure you have found this. I don't suppose for one moment that you conduct all your interviews in exactly the same manner, do you? Some need persuading or coaxing, others perhaps even . . . bullying? Well, I'm the same. Many of my sheep don't need watching over. Many would resent it. Some people wander off the path and need only a little reminder, others you have to press and press and press.'

'And what category did Miss Masters

fall into?' said Townley. 'I think you told the Sergeant you thought she needed . . . nudging? That was the word wasn't it . . . nudging?'

'Yes, that sounds correct,' said Father Johnston.

Townley pounced. 'Then why was it taking so long, why visit after visit for this one woman who had only been inside your church just the once?'

The priest's hand went to the telephone on the desk. He put his hand on the dial, his finger in one and dialled it. He did this again and again, before he turned his attention back to Townley.

'I believed she could be saved,' he said. 'I was confident I could save her and bring her to the Lord. If you like it was a challenge. It was the Lord who said: 'There is joy in the presence of the angels of God over one sinner who repents.''

'It's the one sheep that's lost, then, is that it?' said Townley.

Father Johnston looked at him a little longer. 'You know that parable, Superintendent?' he asked.

'I've heard it mentioned,' Townley

muttered through his embarrassment. He coughed loudly, wished he had never heard about the bloody sheep, and resumed the offensive.

'Tell me about last Sunday morning,' he said. 'What made you go to see Miss Masters that particular day?'

'I don't know,' said the priest. 'The spirit moves in strange ways, and it moved me that morning to go and see her. I hadn't seen her for a while, it was a pleasant morning, and I thought I'd walk round. I remember Mr. Rogers was at the front of the house, painting the door as I recall. I don't think I said much more than 'Good morning' and went on in.'

'What time would that be?' said Townley.

'In all honesty, I don't know, not exactly,' said the priest.

'All right,' said Townley. 'Roughly.'

'Well, let me work it out,' said Father Johnston. 'Mass finished just before eleven. Old Mrs. Dean kept me a few minutes afterwards, about a visit we are making to the hospital next month. I took off my robes, put on my jacket, left church I should say around quarter past eleven. I reckon about a half hour walk to Latrigg — so I'd say I was there around quarter to twelve.'

'Mr. Rogers says twenty to. Would you disagree with that?'

'How can I? I didn't look at my watch as I entered the house.'

'Right,' said Townley. 'What did you do then?'

'I went straight up to the first floor to Miss Masters' door, and knocked on it,' said the priest with a sigh.

'Loudly?'

'Dear me, Superintendent, I can't remember THAT.'

'Why not?' said Townley. 'She didn't answer, did she? Presumably you knocked more than once, and if you're like the rest of the population, each knock gets louder than the one before. How many times did you knock?'

'Superintendent, if I'd known you were going to ask such questions a week later, I would have taken due note. I would have written them down. Exact time of arrival. Exact time of departure. Number of knocks upon the door, number of steps upon the stairs. And I've no doubt, if I'd so desired, I could have found some machine for measuring the density of noise as I banged my knuckles against the door. As it is . . . I DON'T KNOW. I would say I knocked twice, may be thrice. Does all this matter? Or is there some hidden meaning behind the question? If I say I knocked twenty times, each louder than the last . . . then why didn't anybody hear me? Got you Johnston!'

It was Townley's turn to sigh. He abhorred questioning Clever Dicks. Give him the George Harts of this world, who took each question at its face value and didn't try to see beneath it or beyond it, but answered it.

'And when you came to the conclusion that you weren't going to get any answer, what did you do?' he said.

'Ah,' said the priest, leaning forward, his finger pointing at Townley. 'Then I wrote the incriminating note.'

Townley broke in. 'Look here,' he said. 'This is a matter of murder. It's serious, and I've got to find out who committed this crime. Questions I've got to ask, and questions I'll bloody well ask, whether you like 'em or not, whether you can see any sense in 'em or not. Now, what did you do when she didn't answer the door?'

Good, thought Father Johnston. He's rattled. Authority in this room, in this house, belonged with him, not the police. 'I would remind you where you are, Superintendent, and ask you to moderate your language, if you don't mind. And an apology wouldn't come amiss.'

Townley nearly exploded. 'APOLOGY,' he shouted. 'APOLOGY. Don't get on your high horse with me, Father Johnston. I wouldn't apologise to you if my very life depended on it. Let's just get a point or two straight shall we. I've got a lot of people to see, a lot of questions to ask. I get tired of the 57 varieties of people I have to deal with, all the flotsam that's thrown up on the beach of Rosedale. MURDER is what I'm here about, and I represent the law. And how I piece this bleeding jig-saw together is my business. I haven't time to waste on niceties nor on damn-fool questions, whatever you might think. Now let me clear up the question of last Sunday morning . . . then Father, we'll get along to the Blue Elephant.' He gritted his teeth and hissed out the next question: 'What, Father Johnston, did you do when there was no answer to the door?'

The priest glanced out of the window, then started fiddling with the phone again. 'I wrote the note that you found behind the door.'

'It's a very short note,' said Townley. 'How long did it take you to write it?'

'I don't know. A few minutes. As I've said, I had to weigh very carefully what I wrote.'

'And when it was written what did you do?'

'I pushed it through the letter box. Then I left the house.'

'You didn't see anybody else, you didn't knock on anybody else's door, but you went down the stairs and back out through the front door?'

'That's right.'

'Then WHY were you in there half an hour?'

'I'm not sure it was that long.'

'Mr. Rogers is sure. Very, very sure,' said Townley.

'Ah yes, Mr. Rogers. Then it must have taken me a good deal longer to compose my note than I realised.'

'Father Johnston, are you telling me you could have spent between 25 and 30 minutes composing it, and not known about it?'

'It must have been like that.'

Townley fished the note out of his pocket. ''Doreen,'' he read. 'Did you always call her Doreen. Not Miss Masters?'

'Yes, I knew her pretty well.'

'Mmmm . . . 'Doreen, I called to see you this morning, but unfortunately I could get no reply. I assume you were out. At least I hope you weren't avoiding me.'' Townley stopped reading, and let the words sink in. 'Why would she avoid you?' he asked quietly.

'I wasn't really suggesting she would,' said the priest. 'I was just making a funny.'

'You don't think perhaps she was fed

up of your persistence?' said Townley.

'She'd never given any hint of that. She was a straightforward girl, outspoken. If she hadn't wanted to see me any more she'd have said so.'

'Were you persistent?' asked Townley.

'I suppose I was.'

'Maybe . . . TOO persistent?'

'And what is that supposed to mean, Superintendent?'

The two men looked at each other eye to eye, like two schoolboys staring one another out, neither being the first to blink.

It was Townley who broke the spell. 'If you had seen her, would you have told her all about the Blue Elephant, Father Johnston?'

18

Father Johnston said nothing for a few moments. He looked out of the window and could just make out, through the rhododendrons, a woman in a white raincoat slowly making her way up the avenue. He watched her, ignoring Superintendent Townley as if he weren't in the room.

Superintendent Townley said nothing more. He was applying quiet to an interview again. Jones had obviously been right. Father Johnston had been to the Blue Elephant. He was in a tight spot and it must have been taxing his conscience severely as to the right way out. Townley reached for a cigarette, lit it, and looked around for an ash-tray. There was one lying in the fireplace, nice enough to be an ornament, nearly big enough to be a fruit bowl.

He noticed a photograph on the mantelpiece. It was a girl, her face bright and alive, her eyes shiny, not a scrap of make-up, an attractive, healthy, outdoor type.

'My sister,' said Father Johnston. 'Geraldine. I'm the oldest of the family, Geraldine's the next.'

Superintendent Townley made no comment. He glanced at the priest and back to the photograph. There was a likeness, around the mouth, a humorous mouth that probably laughed a good deal. Father Johnston was not laughing now. He continued to stare at Townley, and then said: 'Have you been to the Blue Elephant?'

'Yes, I have,' said Townley.

'Were you on duty?'

'Policemen, priests, reporters, doctors — they're never off duty, not if they're doing the job properly. Their work is happening all the time, it's all around them, and if they involve themselves in their work, they can never get away from it. Life is our business, Father Johnston.'

'Precisely,' said the priest.

'And what's that supposed to mean?' asked Townley.

'We — you and I — have to involve ourselves in life. We have to see every side of life, not just the good, but the bad as well. What sort of a priest would I be if I only concerned myself with the people who attended church, if I kept myself forever surrounded by a cotton-wool cushion of good living. This is where the church has become lost through the years. It hasn't concerned itself enough with all aspects of life, it has been too narrow, too involved in its own little happenings. We need to see how the other half lives, it is important that people see us in a multitude of environments, not just in church fetes and mothers' unions, at mass and confession.

'For too long the clergy have been cushioned against the sordid happenings of the world. We have avoided too many of them as if we have been afraid to soil our hands with the dirty parts of this life. But we HAVE to get closer to it. To appreciate people's problems, it is better if we have experienced them. We need to KNOW how our people are thinking, we need to LIVE with them more, to experience the things that they experience.'

'What you're trying to say,' Townley chipped in, 'is that there's real value for a priest in watching a stripper taking her undies off in front of a cheering, panting set of fellas.'

'That's not a very nice way of putting it,' said Father Johnston.

'It's not a bloody nice thing to do,' said Townley.

'I really must protest at your language,' the priest declared.

'Oh do give over,' said Townley. 'Don't give me all that eyewash about having to live the way the peasants live. I'm all for watching a woman's brassiere come off myself, nothing better, but don't, please don't, put it on the same social footing as visiting the sick and the aged.'

'Don't you lecture me, Superintendent. I don't have to explain myself to you.'

'Oh yes you do,' said Townley. 'Now that's just where you're wrong. That's where you're totally mistaken. You DO have to explain to me. There's been a murder, and according to my information, you might very well have been the last person to have seen Doreen Masters alive. And when I find a priest frequenting a strip joint in Manchester, renowned for its filthy comics and its filthy strippers, I want to know just how far the frustrations of celibacy drive a man.'

'Don't you throw your insults around here, Superintendent,' cried Father Johnston, who still managed to retain the courtesy of the Superintendent's title through all the accusations. 'I've told you what I was doing there, and you can think just what your dirty little mind wants you to think. And I'll say it again if it will help. I went to the Blue Elephant simply because it is life at its most sordid. I NEED to know about every aspect of life, whatever it is like. I've been down mines as well, you know, I've been in sewers, I worked a day as a dustman, I've been in the cotton mills.'

'Well now,' said Townley, 'And do they take their underclothes off there as well?'

'I've no more to say, Superintendent. I've answered your rude, insulting, personal, persistent questions, and now I'll be glad if you'll leave.'

'Not yet,' said Townley. 'How many times have you been to the Blue Elephant, or any other strip club, come to that?'

Father Johnston pushed his hand wearily through his hair, then got hold of the bridge of his nose between finger and thumb, pressed hard, and closed his eyes. He breathed in deeply three times, gathered himself, and gave his attention once more to the policeman.

'Several times. I don't know exactly,' he said tiredly.

'And how many times have you been down a mine?'

'Once.'

'A sewer?'

'Once.'

'And one day as a dustman I think you said.'

'Yes.'

'How many days in the mill?'

'One.'

'Then why did it need so many visits to get to know the workings, to understand the feelings of people in a strip club?'

The priest closed his eyes again, leaned his head back on his chair, but said nothing.

'Could it be,' said Townley quietly, 'that you enjoyed it?'

'No it wasn't,' the priest cried. 'It was repulsive. I've told you, I just wanted to experience what other people experience.'

'And you expect me to believe that?'

'Believe what you like. That's why I was there.'

'Does anybody at your church know you've been to the Blue Elephant?'

'No, I haven't told anybody.'

'Why not, when you consider it part of your duty? Were you ashamed?'

'A little, I suppose. But I don't think it necessary for me to tell everyone everything that I do.'

'What do you think they'd say at the church if they knew? Do you think they'd believe this nonsense about seeing life at first hand?'

'People will believe what they want to believe, Superintendent,' said Father Johnston. He had regained his composure once more and could think clearly enough to philosophise. 'There are those in the congregation who would see it for what it was, a genuine attempt to see life as it is. And there are those, like you, who would not believe a word of it, and would put the worst possible conception to it. I don't know how many would understand, or try to understand my motives, but I hope I am big enough to do what I see is right, regardless of what people think. A priest has always to follow his conscience, follow his God, and trust in God to make people understand his reasons. I cannot be responsible for people who cannot, or will not, see what is there in front of them. My conscience is clear.'

'And what do you think the Bishop would say if he heard about the cavortings of a young member of the priesthood?' asked Townley.

'I believe the Bishop has enough faith in me to know that what I do, I do with God in mind. And that no other reason dictates my actions.'

'I think he might find it hard to swallow that God dictates that you should watch a pair of balloon-sized breasts at the Blue Elephant, don't you? Dear me, Father, anybody that will believe that little lot will believe in fairies.'

'Why, don't you?' Father Johnston asked.

'Well, not the sort you might be thinking of,' said Townley.

'Superintendent . . . THAT . . . is a fruit bowl. There is an ash-tray on the table.'

Townley got up, went over to the table, collected a glass ash-tray that probably held salted peanuts at party time, and returned to his seat.

'Do you intend mentioning this?' the priest asked the Superintendent.

'I most certainly do,' said Townley.

'To whom?'

'To the Bishop and the church leaders,' said Townley.

'Why?'

'Are you still trying to tell me you don't know why?' the Superintendent asked.

'Yes, I am.'

'Go on, pull the other one, it's got bells on. I'll tell you why. My job is to protect the public. And I don't believe just from criminals, not only from people who feel compelled to murder, rape, steal, assault, but from people in positions of power who mislead and exploit. Unscrupulous people who take advantage of the weak, immoral people who control our morals. Do I make myself clear?'

Before Father Johnston had time to answer, Townley pursued his argument. 'It doesn't matter tuppence what I do in a strip club — although the wife wouldn't be too delighted — it doesn't matter what the sewage man, the dustman or the miner does in the strip club. But by the hell, it does matter what you do. Because you are a paragon of virtue in our society, you and God set the highest standards which we lesser mortals should all aspire to reach. You are above all this, and where you lead we follow. And if a 'G' string here and a bra there is all right for you, how do we tell our children it's all wrong? What people think of me really doesn't matter. What they think of you is all important. You teach the children of this parish, you put them on the path to

God . . . but I'll tell you what, if I lived in this parish, if I had any children, I wouldn't want them within a hundred miles of you. Cause that's how far I reckon the stink will carry!'

Townley stubbed his cigarette out in the salted peanut bowl as if he were trying to bore a way through it. Rarely had he put out a cigarette with such feeling. When he had finished he got to his feet, and without a glance at the priest made for the door. 'I'll no doubt need to see you again,' he said as he gripped the door handle. He opened the door. 'Best of luck with the sermon,' he said as he went through. He walked down the corridor and just as he reached the front door, Miss Moran appeared from her sitting room off the hall.

'You've finished then?' she said abruptly.

'For the time being,' said Townley.

'Perhaps now he'll be getting on with his sermon without interruption,' she said.

'I think this sermon might take rather a long time,' said the Superintendent. 'And it's one I would dearly like to hear.'

She opened the door, he stepped out onto the drive.

'Clearing up nicely,' he said, looking up at the sky.

There was no answer. The door slammed.

'Bloody big head,' muttered Bridget. 'The likes of him shouldn't be allowed in the same building as the dear Father, God bless him.'

She bustled off down the corridor to make sure the nasty Superintendent had not upset her beloved Father.

19

As the door closed behind Superintendent Townley, Father Johnston crumpled like an old suit. Odd, he could work solidly from seven in the morning until ten at night, and not feel anything like the exhaustion which had overtaken him now. He was spent, utterly, completely fatigued. He couldn't face his sermon now, it would have to wait.

This man had made it perfectly clear that he did not believe a word of his reasons for his visits to the Blue Elephant. Would the Church Council? Perhaps not. And John Hardy, the chairman, as well as being a shrewd old bird, was extremely narrow-minded and wouldn't consider those the actions of a parish priest, whatever the modern reasoning. And the Bishop? He knew he was safe there. As he had told the Superintendent, he believed the Bishop had enough faith in him to know that whatever he would do, he would do with God in mind.

There was a knock at the door, and right behind it, Bridget bounced into the room. Would she never learn to knock, then wait to be invited in? All right, so it was a lifetime's habit of entering any room other than the bedroom, but she really ought to know better.

'Heavens, Father, you look washed out,' she exclaimed. She hurried up to him and peered closely at him. 'Do you feel all right?'

'Yes, thank you, Bridget,' said the priest wearily. 'Not a very pleasant experience dealing with policemen hot on a murder trail. But I'll be all right. I could do with a pot of tea, if you could manage it.'

'For sure I can,' she said. 'Nothing else you want, aspirin maybe, you look proper dragged down.'

'No thank you, Bridget, tea will be fine.'

Bridget bustled back to the door where she turned to look at him again. 'Nasty, nasty man that fellow,' she said.

'Now, now Bridget,' he said. 'Where's your Christian feelings?' But he said it with little conviction. She was right. Not the sort of man you'd want to know.

Bridget left, and hurried to the kitchen to prepare an obviously badly-needed cup of refresher. Lord preserve us, she thought, something had happened in that room. Father Johnston must have had some terrible experience to look like that. He wasn't a man who easily flustered, but you'd only to look at him to know he'd been badly upset. Surely he didn't know anything about the murder. He did know that woman, Doreen Masters, of course, but that wasn't enough to turn him into the physical wreck he had looked two minutes ago.

That policeman must have badgered him something awful. The Superintendent was responsible. But why? Why badger a priest? Surely the police didn't think he had something to do with the murder? Oh, no, they couldn't think that. Not Father Johnston. He wasn't that sort of man. No priest was that sort of man. They had nothing to do with women, except in a purely professional way. Well . . . they *shouldn't* have anything to do with women.

The father was a good-looking man. In a Church of England parish he'd have had all the women flocking around, and not just the single ones looking for a likely husband, either. A good-looking priest had his admirers, too, she knew that from past experiences as well, and Father Johnston did draw them, like thirsty animals to a water hole. But surely he couldn't have been involved with the woman. She filled the kettle, put it on the stove, and got down the small teapot she used exclusively for the Father when he was alone.

No, he was young and fresh, eager in his first parish. Not like some of the old fogies she had seen, who had let the job just tick along, unable to give it some much needed oil from time to time, but content to let one day follow the next. Now THEY might well get unpriestlike urges on occasions, the frustrations of their position might well overtake one or two of them, here and there, in all sorts of funny ways.

She put the tea in the pot, got out the tray with the picture of Ashness Bridge, covered it with a tray cloth of good Irish lace, put the cup, saucer, milk and sugar alongside it. She stood, waiting for the kettle to boil.

But Father Johnston was young. At that age the job meant everything. Well, usually it did. There was no time for anything but the flock and its needs. She thought a bit deeper. Last Sunday morning that nice police sergeant had said. Last Sunday . . . he had come back as usual after mass. She had watched for him. That's right. He wouldn't have tea, he'd said. Going visiting, and straight out he'd gone. And not the first time either. She considered. How long had he been out? She wasn't sure, but he had been there in time for dinner, on the dot at half past twelve. He had been rather quiet, she recalled. But this wasn't unusual among the priests. People's problems became theirs, they took the cares of the world on their shoulders, and long silences weren't uncommon. Still, last Sunday morning . . .

The kettle boiled, she filled the pot which held just enough for two cups, and put some biscuits on to a plate. He was fond of biscuits with his tea. She picked up the tray. Last Sunday morning . . . Doreen Masters . . . murder . . . police . . . no, it was too silly for words.

Father Johnston welcomed the interruption for a cup of tea. His thoughts were carrying him off wildly in too many directions, it was good to see something solid and dependable like dear Bridget. The world was not coming to an end. Not at that minute, anyway. He let her pour out a cup for him, then she stood and stared at him. She had a habit of doing that, not leaving until she was told to. Strange woman. She'd burst into the room without so much as a by-your-leave, but get rid of her? That was a different proposition altogether.

'Thank you Bridget,' he said by way of dismissal.

'No trouble at all sir,' she said without taking the hint, but continuing to stare deep into his blue eyes. Bit watery, she thought. Been welling up.

'Lamb chops for dinner,' she said.

'Beautiful,' said the priest.

'Roast potatoes, cauliflower and carrots.'

'My favourities.'

'I thought you'd like them. And rice pudding.'

Father Johnston felt like the condemned man. All his favourite foods, all at one go. He must look awful.

'I can look forward to that, Bridget. Now, I must get on.'

'Right you are, Father.' She went to the door and turned again, concern written all over her lined face. 'Don't let it worry you,' she said. 'It will all look different in the morning.' She went out and back to her kitchen.

Father Johnston stirred his tea, an unnecessary action after the prolonged whisking Bridget had given it, but he had to get his hands moving on something. Anything, but complete stillness. Nervousness, but then he had something to be nervous about.

What would his mother and father think? They who had encouraged and helped him towards the priesthood, who had been so proud when he had chosen the church as his life. Some parents would have tried to dissuade him, but not them. He could still see his mother's face the day he had told her. He was 16, but he had known for months what he wanted. He felt he had known all his life. Her face had broken into the biggest smile he could ever remember. It had split right across like a boiled egg cracked open. The smile turned to a laugh, then tears had run down her cheeks as she had embraced him in delight. And not a word had she said. She hadn't needed to. Her feelings were all in her face. Words weren't necessary. His father, too, had been delighted. He had jerked his arm up and down. 'Suited' he'd said he was. He'd always remember that. 'Well, I am suited, Joseph,' he'd said.

The priest sipped the hot, strong, sweet tea. Goodness. There must be four spoonfuls in there. Bridget must think he'd had a big shock to need tea like that. She was probably right. He drank some more.

What would he do? He had grown with this parish, not a big one, not specially flourishing, but it was growing, and he had become attached to it. No policeman was going to drive him out, not even a Detective Superintendent. But clearly, the next few days were going to be uncomfortable. If he was any judge of people, the Superintendent WOULD keep to his promise, he would tell the church authorities. And if he didn't, somebody else knew, and the word would get about.

'Bloody hell and damnation,' he shouted.

Just as the last word was out of his mouth, a knock at the door, and in burst Bridget. 'Did you say something, Father?' she asked, looking round to see if any little ghost had crept in while she wasn't looking.

'I did, Bridget, I did. But it's not fit for the ears of a priest's housekeeper. What did you want?'

'John Hardy, Father. He's here. Wants to see you. Says it's most urgent.'

20

Superintendent Townley walked slowly down the drive, gaily humming a piece of Gilbert and Sullivan, and shaking his head in tune with the music . . . 'For the merriest fellows are we, Tra La, Ta tiddly, tiddly, pom pa pom, mmmmmmmmmm.' The Gondoliers. Magical music, sheer magic thought Townley.

He opened the door of his car, squeezed in and pulled the door to. For a few minutes he sat there, smiling to himself, pleased with his little performance with the priest. That should get things moving, he thought to himself. He lit a cigarette and contentedly pulled on it. He had enjoyed that encounter. You're a sadistic sod, Townley, he thought to himself. Poor fellow there, a strong candidate for murder, and if not that, he'll soon have his name bandied round every bar and every living room in Rosedale as the Father of the Strip Clubs.

Poor fellow be buggered, thought Townley. He believed that every man chose his own road in life. He could take the easy one, straight and fast like a motorway, well surfaced with hardly a ripple all the way. He could have the tortuous country lane if he wanted, pleasant surroundings, but a prospective heart attack round every bend. But whatever road you chose, you accepted its laws, its good as well as its bad. If a guy wants to be a priest, bloody good luck to him. But he's like the doctor . . . if you're going to get up to any hanky panky then make damn sure you don't get caught. Because if you do get caught, there's no use complaining. It's no good squealing. You've made your bed. Now lie in it. Lumps and all. Don't expect protection, especially from a Detective Superintendent.

Pride stirred within Townley's vest, he pushed up in the seat as far as the roof would allow, and started the engine. The car ticked over smoothly as Townley considered his route to Len James's house in Monmouth Avenue. The quickest way

. . . up Maynes Avenue, past the cemetery, down Robins Lane — where that woman had that infernal Great Dane, called Mooch — and then down by the Jolly Butcher.

It was a pleasant enough neighbourhood, plenty of greenery and trees, a feeling of country and quiet. Townley's car screamed to a halt outside number 63. He looked out at the purple door, purple gate, purple garage. Hells bells, he thought. Fancy living across from that. He looked back across the road at number 54, a bright, striking orange, piped with yellow like some exotic bird.

Mrs. James opened the door, and Townley introduced himself. 'Len?' she said. 'He's just having a bath, but if you like to come in and wait, I'll tell him you're here.'

Townley was taken into the front room, Mrs. James leading the way, tidying up as she went along, a newspaper off this chair, a dirty dinner plate off another, some brief particles of lingerie draped over the back of the couch. She made for the door, her arms full of papers, pants, slippers, socks, ash-trays, plate, knife and fork in her hands. 'Haven't had a minute for tidying in here,' she said, breathlessly. 'I was just meaning to go over it. Woman's work, you know . . . '

'I haven't got long,' said Townley. A backside like that wasn't worth wasting time on. 'You'll tell your husband won't you? I've a great deal to do. I would like to see him now.'

The emphasis on the word now brought an even brighter glow to Rhoda James's cheeks. Her chin and bosom jutted out challengingly. Arrogant oaf. Let him wait. 'I'm sure he'll be just as quick as he can,' she said in a tone that implied exactly the opposite.

She strutted out of the room and Townley stood there, his hands deep in his trouser pockets and looked around. Television. Soon be the football results. He went over to switch on, studying all the knobs in turn until he found the volume knob. Colour, too. It used to be something to have a telly at all, now everybody was getting colour. And they said there was no money about, the country in a dreadful state. Rubbish, thought Townley.

He sat down and waited for the set to warm up. A racing commentary was galloping from the screen and a few seconds later the picture appeared. It was a re-run of the big race. Townley leaned forward. He'd backed Slice of Luck in this race, a fiver on the nose. Forgotten all about it, he had, in the excitement. 'And now it's Joker's Wild leading from Happy Dance,' the commentator rattled out. 'Joker's Wild and Happy Dance, but here comes Slice of Luck on the outside making a strong challenge . . . '

Townley clenched his fists in excitement. 'Come on Slice of Luck, Slice of Luck,' he shouted.

With a furlong and a half to go, Mrs. James reappeared through the door, walked straight to the television, switched it off and said: 'Mr. James will be here directly.'

Townley was speechless. The whiteness on his knuckles stood out against the red of the chair arm.

'Can't abide 'orses,' she said. ''Orrible.

Them ’orses.’ The door had closed behind her before Townley managed to speak. ‘Not half as ’orrible as yours’ he shouted.

Rhoda James had not heard. At least she did not return to the sitting room, but left Townley to while away the time, waiting for her husband.

Townley looked around and saw the Rosedale Advertiser and the Daily Observer lying on the poufee in the corner of the room, missed by the vigilant woman of the house, still lying where they had obviously been thrown.

The Advertiser was the town’s weekly paper, published on a Saturday. Townley had looked at it this morning before he had left the house, the news part of the paper anyway. Important for a town, its own paper. But you had to be careful with it. It needed more detail than the evening or daily paper, and could easily offend without intention.

Townley turned to the advertisements, births, marriages, and deaths. ‘Hatches, matches, and dispatches,’ his mother used to call them. When he was younger, he had started looking at Engagements and Marriages, then it was the Births. Now he looked first at the Deaths. Another sign of growing old. Like children standing on buses for you, police constables looking younger, taking twice as long to wash your face as there became more of it. And he could never resist those In Memoriams and Birthday Memories and Acknowledgments. What a fortune papers made out of people's miseries. It was bad enough dragging out somebody's death year after year remembering the poor sod, but now they'd actually got round to remembering him on the day he would have been having his birthday. 'Loving birthday memories of my dear husband Charlie, 72nd birthday.' Would it still be there in fifty years time? 'Loving birthday memories of my dear grandad, 122 today.'

He threw down the Advertiser and picked up the Daily Observer. The Prime Minister's smiling mug on the front page again. Exports up or some such nonsense. Wonder how that dog went on last night? He had been told to watch it. Glendon

Rover, running at Salford. He turned to the greyhound results on the inside back page. Sheffield, Leeds, Doncaster results. What interest were they? Where was Salford? He looked on the back page, but no luck. Inside again. No, just those three in Yorkshire. Don't know what the papers are coming to. He settled back to read an interesting-looking article on Tom Finney and Stanley Matthews . . . now those lads could play football.

Football wasn't the same these days — not for the coppers, either. Used to be good-humoured crowds when he was a constable on the beat, now they were vicious, bad tempered, looking for trouble.

He was just settling into the armchair and the article when Len James, his hair wet and plastered to his head, his dressing gown clutched to him, came in through the door. The dressing gown had a hood, and the man was in his bare feet, reminding Townley of a monk.

'Superintendent Townley, isn't it?' said James with a huge grin. 'Len James. Pleased to meet you. What is it you want?'

'The result of the 8.27 at Salford last

night,' said Townley, throwing the newspaper on to the still-cluttered coffee table. 'That paper doesn't give it. Sheffield, Barnsley, Doncaster dogs, but no Salford. Can't see the point of that.'

'Well, that paper there is one of the Yorkshire editions,' explained James, quick to jump in to the rescue of his own newspaper. 'They are all editionised to try to give everybody their own local results and reports. That's why when you go to Scotland you get all Scottish news, and if you go to London you get London news.'

'Well, what's a Yorkshire edition doing here?' asked Townley.

'I work for the Observer,' said James with a suggestion of pride in his voice.

'Oh yes, I remember George Hart saying,' said the Superintendent. 'That's why I'm here. It's about a murder that occurred at Latrigg House about a week ago. Hart tells me he was with you for a good part of last weekend.'

'Well, we didn't see him at all last Saturday,' said James.

'And the Sunday?' said Townley. 'I have good reason to believe the murder happened last Sunday. You and Hart were together that day, I understand.'

James laughed. 'Funny you should say that, Superintendent. George was in here not so long ago, telling us about the murder. I said then he might need an alibi, but he'd know where to come if he did.'

'Did you now, Mr. James? And what exactly did you mean by that?'

'Nothing. Nothing at all, Superintendent. Just a bit of fun, you know. We'd been out together fishing on Sunday, and I thought it might be important. No, I didn't mean anything. Just a joke.' But the smile had gone from Len James's face. A worried expression had replaced it. This was a serious matter, not a time for the pub banter at which he was such an expert.

Townley was silent for a moment as he stared at James. James's face was now a bright red, like a pillar box. Maybe the after-effects of a hot bath, maybe not . . .

'When did you arrange this fishing expedition?' Townley asked.

'Some time the previous week,' said

James eagerly, anxious to atone for his indiscretion. 'Can't remember when. We often went together. We're both members at Mayhurst, and we go to Hard Booth reservoir quite a bit.'

'Is that where you went last Sunday?'

'That's right.'

'And where did you meet Hart?'

'We arranged to meet at Birchill. I got there first, about quarter past eight — that's the time we'd arranged — and George was right behind me.'

'Did he have a newspaper with him?'

'Paper? Yes, he did, the Chronicle. He read the weather report out from it.'

'From Birchill, did you go straight to the reservoir?'

'Well, we set off like, but halfway there George, gormless George, remembers he's forgotten his flies. So we have to go back to his place for them. It wasn't that far out of the way really, but it's typical of him. He drives you mad some times.'

'So you went back. Now how long were you at the house. Did you go in with him by the way?'

'No, not me,' said James with a look of

distaste. 'Can't abide the place. Rambling old house. And all the doors are shut. Too impersonal for me. When I go through a front door I like to think I'm in a house, not being faced with more locked doors. No, it's all right for some, you know, but not my sort of place though. I always meet George outside somewhere now. How long was he in? Funny thing that,' he added.

'Why?'

'Well flies isn't the sort of thing any angler is likely to misplace. I mean an angler knows where his fishing tackle is, all of it. Yet I reckon George must have been in there between twenty and thirty minutes. When he came back I asked him if he'd had his dinner as well while he was there. Snapped my head off he did. Just over a few flies. Not like him at all. Still, what I say is, we can't be on top form all the time now, can we?'

'Some of us have to be,' snapped Townley. 'Did he say what he'd been doing?'

'No. He just sat there quietly and I didn't pursue it. He was like that all day

. . . must have been the bad start we'd got off to. Some days are like that.'

'And did he have the flies with him?'

'Course he did. That's what he went back for, weren't it?'

'Was it?' said Townley. 'And the newspaper? Was that still with him?'

'The Chronicle you mean?'

'That was the paper you said he had, didn't you?'

'Yes, that's right. The Chronicle. No, as a matter of fact, he didn't. Borrowed mine while we were fishing. I said to him: 'Where's yours then?' 'Must have left it behind,' he said.'

'In the flat?' asked Townley.

'I assume so.'

'Would you say George Hart is the forgetful sort?' Townley demanded.

'A shade vague you might say,' said James. 'Forget his head, he would, if it were loose.'

'But it isn't,' said Townley.

'What?'

'His head.'

'What about his head?'

'It isn't loose.'

James laughed. 'I wondered what you were driving at,' he said. 'Well, if you ever do see a headless man, you can bet your last penny it'll be George.'

'Have YOU ever met Doreen Masters?' Townley threw in the question unexpectedly. James looked as shaken as if he had been pushed into Hard Booth reservoir. 'What? Doreen Masters? The girl that was killed. That's right, George said that was her name. Doreen Masters. Met her once. That's right. George mentioned it. I called for him one day and she was coming out of her room. Introduced us he did.'

'I thought you said you didn't go to Latrigg House. Didn't like the place?' Townley was back in the courtroom.

'Quite right,' said James, whose face, which had only just returned to its normal colour, started to redden again. 'That was the only time I was ever there. The only time I'd been in — and I met her. Oh yes, only the once.'

'What did you think of her?' Townley followed up.

'Nice girl,' said James non-committedly.

'Oh, yes, a nice girl like. Very friendly.'

'And how many times do you say you ever saw her?'

'Once, Superintendent. Just the once. Dear me yes.'

'And how well did George know her?'

'Not as well as he'd have liked. He had rather a fancy for that young lady.'

'Did he get anywhere?'

'Not as far as I know. But he's not one to give up easily isn't George. All the world loves a trier they say.'

'He told you about it, did he?'

'Well, just in passing as you might say. We'd have a bit of a joke about it, you know. I knew he fancied her and I'd lead him on a bit, and I could see him getting worked up just thinking about her. Just a bit of fun like.'

'You like a bit of fun don't you, Mr. James?'

'Yes, indeed, Superintendent. What would life be like without a bit of fun here and there?'

'A bloody sight more peaceful, Mr. James. And a lot more simple for the coppers of this world.'

Len James said nothing. He wished this man would go, then he could get dressed. He wasn't the sort of man for sitting around in his dressing gown. He was getting cold anyway.

He leaned forward and switched on another bar of the electric fire. That silly log-fire effect might look warming, but it did nothing for your bones. Fires were meant to warm you. Not look decorative.

Townley hadn't finished yet. 'Would you say George Hart was a bit of a one with the girls?'

James puffed out his cheeks and made a loud popping noise with his mouth. 'You could say that.'

'I'm not saying anything,' said Townley. 'I don't know the fellow. Would YOU say he was fond of the girls?'

'All right, yes. And what's wrong with that?'

'You're putting more words into my mouth, Mr. James. I didn't suggest there was the least bit wrong with it.'

'It was the implication.' James was fed up with the innuendoes, the roundabout questions. Why didn't he just ask him if he thought George could have killed Doreen Masters, right out, man to man, in a straight forward manner, instead of all these suggestions.

'Do you think George Hart could have killed this girl?' Townley rapped out.

James's head shot up. One minute he was looking at the fire, a thousandth of a second later it was the Superintendent's dark brown eyes he was studying.

'What sort of a question's that?' he said defensively. There was more firmness, although a touch of whining, about his voice now. 'How would I know? Fancy asking me a thing like that, about a friend of mine, do I think he could have killed a girl like that? Why don't you ask him? You'll be asking me next. Anyway, he found her, didn't he? Not likely to do that is he, if he's killed her?'

'He was bound to find her today, whether he killed her or not,' said Townley patiently. 'She's the lucky one gets her windows cleaned every Saturday.'

'Even so,' said James sulkily, holding his hands out to the fire. 'Still, not the sort of thing to do.'

'Just answer me this Mr. James. Would you say he had enough time to do it last Sunday morning when he went back for his flies?'

'Time? Course he had TIME. I mean how long does it take to kill somebody? If he'd only been two minutes, it would still have been TIME for him to kill her, wouldn't it? And if you think it through reasonably, if he had intended killing her, he wouldn't have taken 20 or 30 minutes about it. He'd have been quick, wouldn't he, so I wouldn't notice he'd been long away.'

'True,' said Townley. 'But he did have time and you did say he became morose and quiet after he'd been back.'

'Maybe he'd dropped a bottle of milk,' suggested James.

'By the way,' Townley continued. 'How long did you stay at the reservoir?'

'All day. We always do. Till it starts to get dark. That would be, what, around half past eight.'

'And what did you do then? Where did you go?'

'I dropped George off at home, then I went for a pint.'

'Why didn't he go with you?'

'Don't know. Said he didn't feel like it. Said he wanted to go back. Tired, if I remember.'

Townley looked at Len James. He looked a pint man. A pub bore, he thought. Thought of himself as the life and soul of the party, first with the latest joke, then he'd tell it over and over, forget he'd already told it you five times, and tell it again. And he wouldn't stop because he remembered he'd told you. But because nobody was laughing at it any more.

Townley levered himself out of his chair.

Good, thought James, who leaned forward to turn off the electric fire. He unplugged it as well before he looked towards the door where Townley was standing. 'I'll see myself out,' said Townley as he closed the door.

'Bloody great . . . ' James was saying when the door opened and Townley's head came through.

'You did suggest it. I meant to ask, but I forgot . . . ' he said.

'Yes.'

'Did you kill that girl?'

21

It was around 5.15, about the same time that Superintendent Townley was driving away from the James household, that Detective Sergeant Stuart Newman entered the flat that had once been the home of Doreen Masters, bank clerk with Barclays.

She had been on holiday last week. Newman had established that with a phone call to the manager.

'Miss Masters? Yes, yes, that's right. Holiday. Spring holiday. Don't know if she had intended going anywhere. You'd have to ask one of her colleagues. What are all the questions for Sergeant. What has she been up to?'

One of the most distasteful parts of a policeman's life was in having to break the news of a death to the next of kin. Experience gradually hardened you to it, but it was a task you could never do quite dispassionately. There was that horrible moment when the door opened, and you spoke the first word towards telling, perhaps a mother, that her six-year-old son had been run over and killed by a bus.

One woman had become wildly hysterical when Newman had broken the news to her. She had screamed and screamed and ran down the path to the gate. Neighbours had come quickly from adjoining houses, but it was several minutes before the woman could be calmed down. Then she had simply sobbed. A policeman was brought closely into contact with the harsh world of reality, experiences that soften as well as harden a man.

Yet it was different again breaking the same news to somebody not so closely connected. Like colleagues at work. Newman hated to admit it, but there was a pang of satisfaction in bringing tidings, however bad, to a person with only loose ties to the deceased.

'She's what? Murdered? How? My God! When? Do you know who did it? And she was such a pleasant, friendly girl.

Not an enemy in the world.'

It was amazing, Newman reflected, how many people without enemies were murdered.

In contrast to Superintendent Townley's method of interviewing, Newman could positively be described as smooth. He was like milk chocolate.

He thought that much of his attitude in questioning people had developed in sharp contrast to his Superintendent. He was so often appalled by Townley's methods, that he determined he would develop the gentle approach. Polite, kind, smooth, yes, smooth was the word, but for all that, persistent, unyielding, quick to spot and pursue an important point.

He had followed this approach with George Hart, who had clearly had a bad time with the Superintendent. The first thing Newman noticed about him when he opened the door of the flat was his extremely subdued manner. The Superintendent had hardly got out of the front door after their experiences with Mr. and Mrs. Jones, when Newman decided to tackle the window-cleaner-cum-fisherman.

Hart opened the door, and leaned against it tiredly as he looked out at Newman. 'I'd like to see you for a moment, Mr. Hart, if I may,' said the Sergeant.

'Yes, of course, come in.' Hart stood back and held the door open for Newman to enter. 'Sit down, please.'

Hart sank into the armchair by the fire. He looked drawn, as if he had not slept for a couple of nights. 'Are you all right?' asked Newman with concern.

'Yes, thank you. Just a bit weary after a session with your Superintendent. Not an experience I would like too often. I see somebody like that, and I don't wonder at innocent men going to prison.'

The police rank closed. 'I'm perfectly sure that Mr. Townley would not pursue a prosecution unless he were convinced of a person's guilt,' he said, springing more to the defence of the Force, than to that of the individual in question.

'Things get out of proportion. They take on a new shape when he gets his hands on them. All right, so I fancied the girl and she didn't want anything to do with me. But I wouldn't murder her for it.'

'Mr. Hart,' said Newman, quietly but decisively. 'A savage murder was committed not 15 yards from this spot and it is our job to find out who is responsible. That is what we are here for. It isn't easy. Lies are told by the innocent as well as the guilty, and Mr. Townley has got to break down all the evidence. If somebody is hurt along the way to finding the killer, it is to be regretted, but it is unavoidable.'

'No, it isn't,' said Hart. 'Oh no, it isn't. What evidence is there that I killed Doreen? Come on, show me a scrap of evidence. I pestered the girl a bit, that's true. Does that make me a murderer? I had a key to her room, but that doesn't mean a thing. So had Mr. Rogers.'

Hart stopped here. He suddenly went quiet and stared into the fire as if gathering his thoughts.

'You told Mr. Townley, I understand, that you went fishing last Sunday,' said Newman.

'That's right.' Hart looked up, trying hard to see Newman properly after the harsh glare of the fire. ‘All day. Left about eight, got back, I suppose, around half past eight or nine o’clock at night.’

‘Didn’t you come back to your flat in the morning?’

‘Yes, I’d forgotten my flies.’

‘Why didn’t you mention that to the Superintendent?’

‘I don’t know. I don’t suppose I got the chance between all his badgering. Anyway, I was back here soon after I left. It wasn’t important.’

‘You get everything ready for a day’s fishing, but you forget the flies?’

‘Now you’re doing it,’ Hart protested bitterly. ‘Suddenly, forgetting something assumes great importance. I forgot some flies and I came back for them. No great mystery, nothing to get worked up about, just a slip of the memory.’

‘And where had you left them?’

‘Where I keep all my fishing tackle. On top of the wardrobe in my bedroom.’

‘So how long would you say you were in the house when you came back for the flies?’

‘Five to ten minutes. No more. I don’t

think I did anything else as well. Might have gone to the lavatory, I suppose.'

'Had you got to the reservoir before you noticed you had overlooked them?'

'No, we were on our way, but we hadn't got there by any means. I could see old Len wasn't too pleased. He didn't say anything, but he gets that hangdog look on his face as if the whole world's trying to upset him.'

'Do you like Mr. James. Would you call him a close friend?'

'Not a close friend, no. But I see a fair deal of him, either fishing or having a drink.'

'Did he come in here with you last Sunday?'

'Len? No. Said he'd wait in the car for me. I was only a few minutes, you know.'

'Did you buy a newspaper last Sunday, Mr. Hart?' said Newman, trying a new line of investigation.

'Yes, I went to the paper shop before I met Len. Got the Chronicle. Always do.'

'What did you do with it?'

'I can't remember. Why?'

'Well, did you take it fishing with you,

or did you perhaps leave it in here when you came back for the flies?'

'I don't know. I like to read the paper when I'm fishing, but when we got up there I couldn't find it. Wasn't in Len's car.'

'Then you must have left it in here.'

'Well, I never found it if I did. Never saw the silly paper after I'd bought it. Had to borrow Len's.'

'Going fishing tomorrow?'

'Heavens, no. I'm in no state. The way I feel, I'll stay in bed all day. It's a good job I didn't stay in bed last Sunday, isn't it?'

'How do you mean?'

'Your Superintendent really would have had something to get his teeth into then, wouldn't he?'

Newman had felt some sympathy for Hart — if he was telling the truth. Innocent people understandably felt aggrieved at pertinent, probing questions, especially when they felt themselves being cornered for no right good reason.

But was Hart telling the truth? Motive and opportunity were certainly there, and he had no doubt that he and the priest were high among the Superintendent's mental list of suspects. The grilling's not yet over, Mr. Hart, I'm afraid. Not by a long way.

Newman left the house after leaving Hart's flat.

'No sign of this other woman, Andy?'

The constable stopped in the middle of his small circular stroll in front of the main entrance. 'No, not yet. She's the only one left, isn't she? I'll let you know as soon as she gets here.'

Newman wandered down to the front gate and looked back at the handsome house. The sort he would like with its own grounds, plenty of room to move and breathe, and nice lawns for sunbathing. Murder was set in some unlikely scenes. And for the next few days it would be the focal point for all manner of people, the curious and the morbid, inquisitive, imaginative people, many of whom would stand and stare, unabashed, as if expecting the entire scene to be replayed just for them. And if the case gathered sufficient notoriety there would be the souvenir hunters as well. He recalled one famous case where an old dear had been murdered, her housekeeper had been found not guilty of her death and had then made figures from the soil and clay of the garden and sold them as souvenirs.

They would come here at night, stealthily, like the old grave-robbers. They'd be happy with a stone, or better still, a flower from the garden. It would be pressed neatly and fondly into a book, no doubt the Bible, and displayed to everybody who set foot in the house.

Newman decided to return to the house and look again at Miss Masters' flat, and as he turned into the front gate, he almost bumped into Mrs. Jones, who was looking at the side of the house.

'So sorry,' said Newman. He wasn't at fault, they hadn't even collided, but he felt an apology of some sort was needed after the dissection of that beautiful cream cake.

'Oh.' Mrs. Jones looked startled and recoiled as if expecting Superintendent Townley to appear from behind Newman's back or up through the ground like a conjuror's rabbit. 'We're just going to the shop,' she explained, although she didn't feel any justification of her movements was called for. 'To get another cake,' she declared.

'I'm terribly sorry about that,' said the sergeant, renowned throughout the station for his competence at pouring oil on the most troubled waters. 'Awful thing to happen. Matter of fact, I'm very fond of cake myself. Specially chocolate with cream on. And my mother makes the most beautiful ginger cake. Tastes lovely with butter on.'

'Has your Superintendent got a mother?' asked Mrs. Jones loftily.

'No, I understand she's been dead many years,' offered Newman.

Mrs. Jones looked away over some larch trees in a neighbouring garden. 'How very fortunate for her,' she said.

Newman decided to change the subject. 'Going anywhere tomorrow?' he asked pleasantly.

'I wish I could,' said Mrs. Jones. 'I don't fancy staying around this place all day. I don't expect to get a minute's sleep tonight you know, but I gather we're not expected to leave. Anyway we've friends coming round.'

'I gather the forecast is quite good for tomorrow,' he said. In truth he had no idea what the weather forecast was for the Sunday, but the situation called for a few cheery words. Spreading light where there was gloom.

'It'll probably pour down all day then,' said Mrs. Jones, apparently resigned to her gloom, and determined to wallow in it.

'Oh, I don't know,' said Newman with a false laugh. 'When you think about it, it really doesn't rain all that much. I mean when you stop to think, really think, how many times are you caught in the rain? I often walk to work and do you know it very rarely rains on me.'

Mrs. Jones greeted this piece of idiotic generalising with a 'Humph' and another look at the side of the house to see if her husband was appearing in the car.

Newman pressed on regardless. 'Still, you're having friends to tea tomorrow, aren't you?' he said. 'That should be nice. I like having friends round. Something very comforting about friends isn't there . . . it's good to have them around you, always gives me a tremendous feeling of satisfaction.'

Mrs. Jones gripped the umbrella she was holding and pointed it at Newman. 'I love having friends round, Sergeant. I like entertaining them. And it's a good opportunity to prepare something nice for tea. Martin's cream cakes are the best in Rosedale. There's nobody makes cream cakes quite like Bill Martin. Our friends like them, too, and Bill saved that one specially for me.'

'Yes, but there's only one piece gone,' said Newman by way of comfort. But as soon as the last word was out of his mouth he knew he should have said nothing.

Gertrude Jones's eyes bore into his. 'That whole cake was contaminated,' she hissed. 'Polluted! There's none of it left. If I'd had a dog I wouldn't have given it to it.'

Just then, Newman heard the sound of a car engine starting up behind the house. Superintendent Townley did say to have a word with Mrs. Jones. Hang it. Superintendent Townley could have his own word with her when he got back.

Words were unnecessary. Newman left and went back into the house and up to Doreen Masters' flat. He got to the door before he remembered that the Superintendent had the key. He would have to go down to Rogers' apartment for another.

The Rogers were just finishing tea. Smelt like they'd had curry. Probably a good hot bindaloo. Newman made a mental note not to get too close to either Mr. or Mrs. Rogers. If there was one thing he couldn't stand, it was second-hand curry.

'I wonder if I could have the key for Miss Masters' flat. The Superintendent's got the other,' Newman explained.

'Of course, of course,' said Rogers. 'Come on in. We're just finishing tea. Like a cuppa?'

'Yes, I would. That would be lovely,' said Newman.

Mrs. Rogers smiled sweetly at the Sergeant. Such a nice young man. Fancy having to put up with that horrid

Superintendent. 'A piece of Wycoller cake, sergeant?'

Newman sat down with his tea and cake, completely at home in this restful room and finding it hard to think that there'd been a murder in the room above.

'Mrs. Rogers,' he said tentatively. 'As you know the police have to check out all statements. Just routine, but it is insisted upon.'

Newman wasn't averse to suggesting that anything distasteful he had to do wasn't anything to do with him. 'It was insisted upon.' Let her think it was the Superintendent's fault. That's what he was paid for. Newman wasn't going to tell her that like any conscientious policeman, he didn't take any statement on its face value, but believed in checking it out as carefully as possible.

'If you could tell me the address of your . . . sister wasn't it? . . . where you stayed last weekend I'd be grateful,' Newman pressed on.

'You're not suggesting Mrs. Rogers had anything to do with this dreadful affair, are you, Sergeant?' said Rogers quickly.

'Of course not sir,' said Newman. 'But as you will appreciate, the first things my superiors want to know about where people were at the time of a murder is . . . were the facts checked. It sounds as if everybody's distrusted. But it is the only way we can work. Everything checked, then we can eliminate.'

'Yes, I know, but God bless us, I've told Mr. Townley I put m' wife on the bus to Buckland after tea last Saturday, and she didn't get back till Sunday evening.'

'Yes sir,' said Newman patiently, 'but I do have to verify it.'

'Gracious me,' blustered Rogers, 'don't know what the world's . . . '

His wife broke in on his protests. 'For pity's sake, stop bothering,' she said. 'He's got a job to do and a not very nice job at times, I shouldn't think. Let's not make it any more difficult for him. My sister's name, sergeant, is Mrs. Edith Green and she lives at 68, Moorcourt Road, Buckland. She's on the telephone, too. Buckland 44678.'

'Thank you very much, Mrs. Rogers. I'm very sorry and I do realise it sounds as if we are accusing everybody of lying. But that's just the way of it.'

'Of course. Another piece of Wycoller cake?'

Sergeant Newman saw no reason to resist such a delicious offering. After all, he was in no immediate hurry, and unlike so many of his colleagues, he wasn't watching his waist line. Slimming, he considered, was one of the big con jobs of the age. The number of people making a living keeping people looking like emaciated straws was fantastic. And all the thin folk he knew were all miserable with it, wishing they could have a piece of this or a drink of that, and almost afraid to smile as if that might put on another pound.

But he knew his manners. He took the smallest piece. 'Not that one,' said Mrs. Rogers. 'Go on, take that big piece, there.'

When he had finished, Newman again thanked Mr. and Mrs. Rogers, and left them to go up to Miss Masters' flat.

The door into the Rogers' flat had just closed behind him, Newman had taken one step up the stairs, when a whispered call, 'Sergeant, Sergeant,' made him turn round. It was Mrs. Shuttleworth. No, Miss Shuttleworth. He remained standing on the bottom step. 'Yes,' he said. 'Could I see you for a moment?' she said.

Newman stepped down, walked back down the corridor and past the old lady, and into her flat.

'Cup of tea, Sergeant?' she asked.

'No thank you madam, I've just had one. What was it you wanted?'

'I thought you ought to know . . . ' she started.

That was usually the prelude, Newman reflected, to a piece of gossip.

'I thought you ought to know,' said Miss Shuttleworth, looking around her as if she expected somebody to appear from behind the curtains, 'about something that happened a couple of weeks ago.

'I'd forgotten all about it, but sitting here this afternoon, and mulling over the murder of that poor girl, I got around to thinking about her and what I knew about her and so on. Such a pleasant girl, always had a smile and a word for you, and I liked to see her around.

'But she was a one with the men, you

know. Anyway, a couple of weeks ago it was, I'd left the door open to let a bit of air in when I heard these footsteps coming down. I thought I'd say hello, it gets a bit lonely when you're on your own all day, you know, when the front door banged, and somebody said: 'You. You're just the person I wanted to see.' It was that old battleaxe from upstairs, Mrs. Jones, and I wondered who she was talking to. It was Doreen Masters on her way out. 'What do you want with me?' she said.

'Well, I couldn't go out then, could I? It would have looked like I'd been there waiting. Not that I'm interested in their business, but when you're in a spot like that, people jump to conclusions, don't they? So I stayed where I was.

'Are you sure you won't have a cup of tea? You're most welcome.'

'No, no thanks,' said Sergeant Newman. 'Do go on, please.'

'Well, this Mrs. Jones starts into Doreen. On at her about her husband. 'If you go near my husband again you'll answer to me for it.' she said. Accused her of trying to seduce him and all sorts of things. Doreen didn't say a word for quite a long time. Then I heard her say: 'Don't flatter yourself, Mrs. Jones, that I would be interested in YOUR husband,' she said. 'I couldn't think of anything more horrible,' she said. 'Just thinking about it sickens me,' she said. Then do you know what she said?' asked Miss Shuttleworth, with a little chuckle.

'I've no idea,' said Newman.

''Mrs. Jones,' she said. 'If I ran a brothel and your husband was the only man to come for a month, I wouldn't touch him with a barge pole.'

'There wasn't a word then for oh, it seemed ages, then I heard this splutter-ing. It was Mrs. Jones. She swore at her. Called her a whore she did. 'You so and so whore,' she said. And she was, like, shouting under her breath. 'Don't you talk to me like that,' she said. 'I know all about you and your men friends. Well, I've told you. You stay away from my husband or I'll sort you out good and proper.' She seemed to go on for a good five minutes, what she would do and what she wouldn't do if she caught her messing around with her dear old Ernie.

'But Doreen had the last word. Funny, she only spoke twice through it all. When Mrs. Jones had run out of steam again, I just heard Doreen say: 'Have no fear, Mrs. Jones. I want nothing at all to do with your husband. I'm only interested in men.' Then the door slammed and the last I heard was Gertrude banging her way upstairs.'

Sergeant Newman considered. Clearly Miss Masters was the sort of woman who attracted men. What sort of men wasn't important. All sorts of men, by the sound of it, which could be very annoying for their wives, especially if they did happen to live in the same building.

'Was there anything between them, do you think?' he asked.

Miss Shuttleworth fussed with the edge of her tablecloth, and without lifting her head looked at the Sergeant demurely from beneath her eyelashes.

'I just wouldn't know,' she said. 'At least nothing definite. They all seemed to try to flirt with her a bit, you know, the way men do. Nothing in it on the surface, just harmless flirtation. If they do happen to strike lucky and the girl does lead them on a bit, then they're all right. But if the girl does turn her nose up and get on her high horse he can always say he was just having a bit of fun. They're like that, men, aren't they?'

'Well, I hope they're not ALL like that,' smiled Sergeant Newman.

Miss Shuttleworth blushed a little and looked embarrassed. 'Of course, present company excepted,' she said. 'But you know what I mean. I should say I've seen all the men in this house trying it on at some time or other. But don't ask me if any of them succeeded. I have my suspicions, but really I don't know anything for sure.'

'Could all the men in the house, Mr. Jones, Mr. Rogers and Mr. Hart, ALL have . . . mmm . . . succeeded . . . ?' asked the Sergeant.

'As I said, Sergeant,' said Miss Shuttleworth. 'I really don't know.' She looked up at the ceiling as if asking for forgiveness as she added: 'But I wouldn't be a bit surprised.'

Sergeant Newman started to head for the door. 'Well thank you Miss . . . '

'One other thing Sergeant while you're here. Will you tell the Superintendent — is he here by the way? No? Well will you tell him I've been thinking about the man I've seen here visiting Doreen. I've thought a good deal about it and I'm pretty sure I'd know him again if I saw him.'

'What man is that?' said Newman.

'Oh, it's one who's been here, I was going to say quite a lot, anyway three or four times recently to see her. He was here last Saturday night and I saw him leave, I think, well after eleven. I heard the door close, then I looked out of the window and saw him going down the drive.'

Interesting, thought Newman. But how would he tie into the case when the murder was committed Sunday morning? Still, it was an important bit of information.

'Obviously nobody you know,' said Newman.

‘No I don’t recollect having seen him before,’ said Miss Shuttleworth. ‘But I don’t get around town as much as I used to. Not so young as I was.’ She smiled. ‘He could live next door and I wouldn’t know.’

‘Yes, I know,’ said Newman. ‘That’s what the motor car has done. We don’t have personal contact like we used to have. Anyway, I’ll tell the Superintendent all that you’ve told me, and thank you for letting me know.’

Miss Shuttleworth walked with him to the door. ‘Did you know I taught the Superintendent when he was a boy at school?’ she asked.

‘No,’ said Newman, surprised. ‘That’s a coincidence.’

‘Yes,’ she said. ‘He was quite a boy, you know.’

‘He’s quite a man,’ said Newman as he left the room.

22

Sergeant Newman climbed the stairs to Miss Masters' flat, inserted the key and let himself in. Not a pretty sight. Somebody was going to have to clean this lot up and that would be an experience in itself.

He stretched himself like a cat, extending his body like a piece of elastic, yawning, and then collapsing like the bag on a carpet sweeper when the electricity is switched off. He sank into the chair and looked around. Newman believed in soaking up the scene of a crime wherever possible, getting the feel of a place as if the walls and floor might speak to him, tell him something to put him on the track of the criminal.

He looked at the television set, switched on to B.B.C. 2. What was on B.B.C. 2 on a Saturday evening? Blowed if he knew, he was an I.T.V. watcher himself, a compulsive Hughie Green and

Ena Sharples fan. There was little on B.B.C. 2 to appeal to his tastes in entertainment.

He had no time to consider the room any further when he heard the key being inserted in the lock. The door opened and Superintendent Townley blew in with the force of a hurricane.

'There you are Newman,' he declared. 'Has this Pertle woman arrived back yet?'

'No sir,' said Newman.

Townley unfastened his jacket buttons, stood hands on hips and looked around him. He had reason to feel reasonably satisfied with his interviews, but little definite was taking shape. It was a horse race with only a few runners, and while he could pick out a favourite, there was no real evidence to support his views.

'Right, tell me what you've learned,' he said to Newman. 'Did you get a word with that Mrs. Jones on her own?'

'No sir, I didn't get the chance. She was in a terrible hurry to get to the shops for another cake before they closed.'

'Another cake?' echoed Townley. 'But there was only one piece gone out of the other one. Plenty left for four people. Funny creatures women though, aren't they? The tea-table won't look the same with a part-eaten cake on it. No, it has to be a new one, a virgin cake, untouched. As if they have to prove to their friends that it was bought specially, just for them.'

'Just so sir,' said Newman. 'But I did get a word with Hart.'

'And what did he have to say for himself?'

'He agreed, sir, that he did return to the house last Sunday morning to collect his flies. Forgot to tell you. Returned soon after he left, and was here only five to ten minutes, he reckons.'

'Five to ten minutes?' Townley echoed again. 'Five to ten minutes. Len James reckons it was nearer half an hour. Hell, five minutes adrift I'll put up with, maybe even ten minutes, but 20 or 25. That's a bit off. What else did he have to say?'

'Nothing of any significance, sir.'

'Did he mention buying the Sunday Chronicle?'

'Yes, he did.'

‘What does he say he did with it?’

‘He can’t remember. He knows he bought it before meeting Mr. James, but when they got to the reservoir, he couldn’t find it. In fact, he never did see it again.’

‘And he called here between buying it and going up to the reservoir,’ Townley mused, not looking for any answer or agreement. ‘Not the sort of discrepancy that shows a mistake. It’s too wide a gulf. Somebody isn’t telling the truth. Another word is called for with Mr. Hart. Anything else before I go to see him?’

‘Yes sir. Dr. Brooks called. The post mortem revealed the deceased was three months pregnant.’

‘Did he now? That IS interesting, Newman. So our flighty Miss Masters slipped up, did she? I wonder who the father was. Wonder if it was somebody here, somebody from this house. Now we have a motive, Newman, we’re getting nearer. Pregnant. Well, well.’

He rubbed his hands together in satisfaction. ‘That is interesting,’ he repeated. ‘A baby on the way. That would throw somebody into a panic, I'll bet. I wonder who?'

'Another thing sir. Miss Shuttleworth caught hold of me.'

'Did she? And what priceless pearl of wisdom had she for the likes of you?'

'A couple of items, sir. One . . . a row she overheard in the hall a couple of weeks ago between Mrs. Jones and Miss Masters. Seems Mrs. Jones tackled the deceased about her husband. As near as doesn't matter, accused her of seducing the man and told her if there was any more there'd be serious trouble.'

'And how did Miss Masters take all this?'

'Gave as good as she got, according to Miss Shuttleworth. Finished the entire interview by telling her her husband wasn't in any danger at all. She was only interested in MEN.'

'Good for her,' said Townley with a leer. 'Wants putting in her place that one, and I don't know that her husband's up to it. And number two?'

'Number two sir? Ah yes. Miss Shuttleworth told you, I believe, about some man who had been seeing a good deal of Miss Masters recently.'

'Yes, seems he was here last Saturday night. At least, that's what she says.'

'Yes sir. Well, she's pretty certain she'd recognise the man if she saw him again.'

'Is she? She wasn't all that certain before. What makes her all that sure now?'

'Said she'd been thinking about it all day, sir. Mulling it over. And now she was fairly certain.'

'Right. Now let's cross the corridor to Mr. Hart.'

'Sir?'

'What is it?'

'Father Johnston sir. Anything new?'

'Quite a lot. There's a few minutes here he can't account for either last Sunday morning when he was writing that note. And the charming Mr. Jones was right.'

'About the striptease sir?'

'Yes siree. And do you know what Father Johnston, son of God, priest in charge of St. Aidan's, had to say about it?' Townley didn't wait for a reply. 'He said that going to strip clubs was all part of getting on the same wavelength as his lay people. He tried to convince me that we're all out watching the strippers night after night, and he, poor fellow, hadn't a clue how the world was getting on. First-hand knowledge, he needed. First-hand knowledge of the depths men will reach so that he can better know how to deal with it.'

'And did you believe him, sir?' said Newman innocently.

'Talk bloody sense Newman,' Townley scoffed. 'He goes to strip clubs for the same reason all we poor bastards go to strip clubs. To get worked up at the sight of some teasing woman, fondly imagining that she's doing it just to us, and that when it's finished we're getting whisked off to some comfortable bed somewhere. When I start to swallow all that crap about finding how the world lives, I'll take my pension and get off to the country,' concluded Townley.

Without another word he opened the door and strode purposefully across the corridor to knock once again on George Hart's door.

Hart visibly sagged when he opened the door and saw Superintendent Townley facing him.

'Another word, Mr. Hart,' said Townley, walking straight into the flat without waiting for an invitation. Newman followed him, smiling wanly at Hart as he passed him, a touch of sympathy in his smile as if he knew every thought passing through Hart's head.

'I've got very little time,' said Townley with the air of a tycoon. 'You didn't tell me you returned to this house last Sunday morning for some of your fishing tackle?'

'I forgot,' said Hart lamely.

'Forgot!' said Townley in an incredulous tone. 'A woman is murdered here last Sunday morning, you come back to collect something you've forgotten, and you forget to tell me?'

'Perhaps if you hadn't badgered me so much I'd have remembered,' Hart threw out. 'It was a wonder I could think of anything. Yes, I came back for my flies. What of it?'

Townley stared at Hart, who was half

sitting on the windowsill. There was new aggression in the man. 'And how long were you here?' snapped Townley.

'I'm sure the Sergeant has told you,' said Hart.

'Well now you tell me,' Townley barked.

'Five or ten minutes.'

'No more?'

'Maybe 15.'

'Sure?'

'Course I'm sure.'

'Could it have been as long as 20 minutes?'

'No.'

'Or half an hour?'

'I've told you, NO. Five or ten minutes.'

'Len James says 20 to 30 minutes?'

'Then Len James is wrong.'

'Or lying?'

'I didn't say that.'

'No I did. He was certain. He was certain because he reckoned you knew where your flies were, and it SHOULD have taken you just a few minutes.'

'Maybe I went to the lavatory,' Hart shouted.

'Can't you remember?' Townley shouted back.

'No I can't. At the time, it wasn't important. At the time, it didn't matter how long I spent looking for flies. At the time, it wasn't important whether I went to the lavatory.'

'But it is now,' said Townley quietly. 'Another thing, that you perhaps overlooked. Your association with the dead woman. As I recall, you told me you had no luck with her, that she wouldn't have anything to do with you. Isn't that so?'

'Near enough yes,' Hart lied.

'Then what about last Christmas? According to Mr. Jones you beat him to the draw. You WERE lucky. Now that's not what you told me, Mr. Hart. Don't tell me. You forgot.'

Hart was on his feet. 'What's Jones know about it?' he blustered. 'He doesn't know. He doesn't know what I did. We had a drink, that's all, for Christmas. That's all,' he lied. 'And he doesn't know any different.' Hart was nearly crying. He was like a child who has been discovered pinching apples.

'But you told me she'd have nothing to do with you. She wouldn't even have a drink with you, you said.' The Superintendent was calm and relaxed, on solid ground as Hart sank further and further into the quagmire he had created for himself.

'That's right,' yelled Hart. 'It was just that it was Christmas. A drink for Christmas. That's all.'

'Nothing more?' asked the Superintendent. 'No sex under the mistletoe? Just for Christmas?'

'No, no, no. Just a drink. One drink. No more.'

'How long ago is that now?' inquired the Superintendent. 'Christmas. How long ago since Christmas?'

'What?' Hart looked startled. 'Three or four months.'

'Three or four months,' Townley repeated. 'How odd.' He turned to Newman. 'How many months pregnant did you say Miss Masters was, Sergeant? Three, didn't you say?'

For a few moments there was silence in the room. Townley stared at Hart, waiting for his reaction. Newman looked at the carpet, a pretty flowered pattern, heavy with blue flowers. Maybe delphinium. Hart stood hunched, head bowed, his eyes closed. He opened them and looked at the Superintendent.

'You think I killed her, don't you?'

'You're a strong candidate,' Townley replied without hesitation.

Hart shook his head. 'You're wrong,' he declared. 'Wrong, wrong, wrong.'

'Did you buy the Chronicle last Sunday?' Townley continued unabashed.

'Not that again,' said Hart wearily. 'Not that now.'

'Yes, that,' said Townley. 'You bought it on your way to meet Len James?'

'That's right. And I lost it.'

'Amazing,' declared Townley. 'You lose yours and there's one in Miss Masters' room we can't account for. Do you remember taking it into the car?'

'Yes, I remember looking at the weather forecast.'

'Did you bring it into the house with you?'

'I can't remember.'

'Did you take it to the reservoir with you?'

'No. When I got there I couldn't find it, so I assumed I'd taken it back into the flat with me here. But I never saw it again.'

'Strange that, don't you think?' said Townley.

'I've lost things before,' said Hart. 'I'll lose things again.'

'You lose one, we find one, and neither of us can account for it,' said Townley.

'Well I didn't put it there,' shouted Hart, his face reddening. 'I didn't see the woman at all that Sunday morning.'

'But you haven't seen your newspaper from that morn to this?'

'No.'

'Amazing. And convenient.'

'Don't be daft.'

'Mr. James said you were very quiet when you got back to the car. Preoccupied, he thought. As if you had something thing on your mind. Had you?'

'Not that I recall.'

'And he says you didn't go for a drink with him that night.'

'That's right. I didn't feel like it. I was

tired. And Len can be a bit much sometimes.'

'But it was unusual, I gather. You not going for a drink after you'd finished fishing,' said Townley.

'I've told you,' said Hart. 'I just didn't feel like a drink.'

'Not your day was it? Forgot your flies, lost your paper, and you didn't feel so good.'

'On any normal day,' said Hart, 'they wouldn't mean a thing.'

Newman felt for this man. Despite his lies or forgetfulness, he didn't think he had committed murder. But he had to be subject to examination, to close investigation, to see if he would weaken, throw out the one mistake they could plant like a seedling and watch it grow and grow into a case. Watertight and certain. But there was nothing certain yet.

'Quite so,' said Townley. 'But on this particular day, in the house in which you live, on the same floor, too, a woman was killed. Anyway, that will do for now. Sergeant.' Townley set off for the door, closely followed by Newman, then by

Hart, anxious to shut out the world for the rest of the day.

Townley turned to Hart at the door. 'Again,' he said. 'How many minutes, top side, were you in here when you came back for the flies?'

'Ten. No more than 15,' said Hart.

'And Christmas? Just a drink?'

Hart nodded.

Townley strode back across the corridor, into Miss Masters' flat once more. 'Thank you,' said Newman, smiling again at Hart.

Hart didn't hear. He was locking the door to his castle. If only he had a drawbridge.

23

'Let's have a look at this again.'

Superintendent Townley and Sergeant Newman were back in the dead girl's flat. The sight and the smell still sickened Townley, but something, somebody, somewhere in this house was going to help him find the killer of Doreen Masters. It was no use sitting in the car, or standing in the drive, it was HERE, all around him, and from HERE he was going to find the answer.

He couldn't sit down. That might suggest he was going to stay a while in this nauseating place, and that was the last thing he intended. He felt better standing, walking around, looking, talking . . .

'Let's have a look at this again. Doreen Masters, stabbed to death here, and found today by George Hart who was cleaning the windows. That reminds me,' he said turning quickly on Newman. 'You told me he was the window cleaner. He works in a bank, you know. Bloody window-cleaner indeed.'

'I wasn't really suggesting that was his occupation,' retorted Newman. 'Simply that that's what he was doing when he discovered the body. Cleaning windows. I never established his occupation. At the time that detail was irrelevant.'

'Like MISSUS Shuttleworth instead of MISS,' snarled Townley. 'Like I said before, Newman, it's all a matter of detail. It IS important.'

'She was your teacher at school, wasn't she sir?' asked Newman innocently.

'What's that got to do with anything?' snapped Townley.

'Nothing . . . just a detail.'

'Well, that's the sort of detail that DOESN'T matter,' shouted Townley. 'Who she taught at school's neither here nor there.'

'Right sir, she just happened to mention that she . . . '

'Never mind,' shouted Townley. 'It doesn't matter where she taught or who she taught. Right? She can stone the front step for all I care.’

‘I only wanted to get the facts right sir,’ said Newman. ‘Detail, you know, sir.’

‘Now don’t you get clever with me Newman. I will establish which details are necessary and which aren’t. Is that understood?’

‘Perfectly sir.’

‘Now, as I was saying. The woman was found here by George Hart,’ Townley looked up again at Newman, ‘who was cleaning the windows.

‘Sunday paper in the flat, obviously brought in. Could have been Miss Masters, but probably somebody else. Priest’s letter and this week’s papers from Monday behind the door. Stop me if I go wrong or don’t make sense. Right, murder committed between paper arriving and priest’s letter being dropped in, always providing the priest is telling the truth.

‘All Sunday morning, from the time the front door is unlocked, the owner, Roger Rogers, is painting the front of the house and sees everybody going in or out. Comings and goings of the regulars, except for Miss Shuttleworth, off to church, and George Hart, returning for his flies, he can't remember. Only one stranger appeared . . . Father Johnston.

'So far so good. There's only one way into the building, the back door is permanently locked, so whoever killed the woman was already inside the building or arrived during the time in question. Am I correct in my assumptions so far, would you say, Newman?'

'Unquestionably, sir.'

Townley looked hard at the Sergeant who didn't flicker an eyelash. Too clever by half that man, thought Townley. You just couldn't tell whether he was making a serious comment or being facetious.

'Could she have been murdered before the time I said, would you say?'

'I'd think not, sir. That would mean the murderer returning with the Sunday newspaper simply to leave it in the room. That seems most unlikely.'

'Right,' said Townley. 'In any case, only Hart and Rogers would have keys to get back into the flat later. Could she have been murdered AFTER Father Johnston dropped his letter in.' This time Townley wasn't asking Newman's opinion. He kept right on talking. 'No, if she'd been out or if she answered the door to somebody, she'd have picked it up. If she was still alive around noon why didn't she follow her usual pattern, out for the milk, and eat the food she had got for Sunday dinner? No, she was dead by dinner time, but alive in the morning to admit the person with the paper. Could she have got the paper herself, then let the murderer in?' Townley asked Newman.

'Unlikely sir.'

'Unlikely,' mused Townley. 'Always a late riser on Sunday. If she had got up early enough why didn't she go to her usual paper shop? No, it all fits. Somebody called Sunday morning, newspaper in hand. She lets him, or her, in, even has a coffee,' he said, waving towards the empty coffee cups. 'Then an argument, temper . . . and murder.'

'The suspects, sir?'

'Suspects. Lets's start at the bottom of the house and work up. Roger and Carmen Rogers. Roger working at the front all morning. Could have done it. There's no reason why he couldn't have been having it off with Miss Masters and put her in the family way. Carmen at his sister's during the relevant time. Has that been checked?'

'No sir. I have the name and address though.'

'Next, Miss Shuttleworth. Opportunity, though no apparent motive. I can't really accept her.

'George Hart, on the same floor as the dead woman. Now he could have done it. There was time on Sunday morning, either before he went out or when he came back for the flies. And three months pregnant puts him well in line from that Christmas caper, whatever he says about only having a drink.

'Ernest and Gertrude Jones. Two more with opportunity. Ernest Jones same motive as Hart. Gertrude had had one row with Miss Masters over some affair involving her husband.

'And Miss Rosalind Pertle, about whom we know exactly nothing at this moment.

'Then there's the one outsider, Father Joseph Johnston, a hot tip for the race. In the house at the opportune time, to all intents and purposes a thwarted, frustrated, sex-starved man who might well have pushed his luck a bit too far.

'Eliminate, I think, Miss Shuttleworth and Mrs. Rogers, and what have we left . . . Rogers, Hart, Ernest Jones, Gertrude Jones, Rosalind Pertle, Father Johnston. Who do you fancy, Sergeant?'

'Blowed if I know sir. Have you a selection?'

'At the moment Newman, I'm torn between priest and window-cleaner. But I don't know . . . I don't know. There's nobody coming through to me clean and clear. There's something missing.'

While he had been speaking, Townley had been walking, pacing back and forth. Now he wandered into the bedroom, then the kitchen, back into the bedroom, and the living room.

He looked at the picture. He liked Breugel, particularly this painting with its contrasts of trees and snow, dark and shining white. He walked over to the table and stood, looking down on the coffee cups, drained almost dry, but stained with a week's waiting to be washed. He picked up the newspaper, the Sunday Chronicle, one of his own Sunday papers, and looked at it again, the front page and the back, all in a few seconds.

He put the newspaper to his lips and continued looking round. Newman stood, respectful, silent, he, too, thinking over all they had learned in a few hours about this murder and the people close to it.

Townley wandered over to the bread knife, dirty red and disgusting, lying on the rug as if it were in a shop window, a priceless item in an antique shop, waiting to be collected. 'It is her own bread knife, I presume,' said Townley.

'I expect so, sir. No finger prints and nothing to suggest otherwise.'

'Not unless her own bread knife is still in the kitchen,' declared Townley. 'Things aren't always as they appear, you know, Sergeant.'

Newman went into the kitchen, Townley stood up from studying the knife, and stared out of the window, seeing nothing, his thoughts of this moment, yet a million miles into space. There was nothing in front of him, his eyes glazed as he floated out into Woodland Road and over the houses. A split second later he was back, his eyes crackled with understanding and light, his face shone with vigour. 'That's it,' he said excitedly. 'Got to be. What a fool I've been. All this time . . . ' He set off briskly to the door, but before he got there, Newman emerged from the kitchen. 'There's no bread knife in there sir,' he said.

But he might just as well have been reading the weather forecast. He could have abused Townley with every swear word in every language in the world. Townley wasn't listening. He was tingling with the exhilaration of his discovery, and he wanted to confirm it now.

'Newman!' He couldn't speak normally any longer. It was a cross between a croak and a bellow. Like a hoarse bull. 'I've got to go,' he said. 'Something to check. Manchester. And give me that woman's address, too, Mrs. Rogers' sister.'

Newman tore the relevant sheet out of

his notebook, and Townley's eager hand snatched it from him. 'Let's see. Quarter past six. Seven, eight, half-past eight, I should be back by then. Get everybody in the house into Rogers' flat, that's the biggest, for then. Say eight o'clock. Better get Father Johnston, and that Len James as well. And another thing.' Townley waved the paper at Newman.

'Sir.'

'Take all their finger prints while you're at it.'

'But we haven't got any prints sir. Not one.'

'What the hell's that matter?' Townley bellowed full throatedly. 'Get 'em.'

He turned quickly and dashed from the room, and Newman heard him descending the steps, two or three at a time. The front door banged, then he heard the soft roar of the Rover engine as Townley scorched down the drive.

This room to front gate, thought Newman. Three seconds. Wonder what's bitten him?

24

Townley headed for the centre of the town, gathering speed, going as fast as he dared down streets that would have been full of traffic and people, an hour, an hour and a half earlier. But this was one of the quietest times of the week, after the afternoon shopping rush, before the start of the Saturday night frolics. He tore down Church Street, touching fifty five miles an hour, blasting his horn with such ferocity that an old couple on their way home from seeing their son dashed into a shop doorway in fright.

'Hooligan,' said Rosalind Pertle who had just come out of the Odeon Cinema. 'The police ought to stop that sort of thing,' she said to her friend, Helen Wright.

Rosalind Pertle, 34 years old, French teacher at Rising Hill Comprehensive School, single but bursting to be married, and as plain as a loaf of bread. But with the help of cosmetics, good clothes, and a splendid carriage, she made the most of the gifts that God and Boots had bestowed on her, and from 20 yards made a most attractive woman. Close-ups, however, did not show her at her best. Close-ups revealed the flaws . . . pointed nose, pointed chin, much more like Punch than Judy, misshapen teeth, and a collection of spots she would willingly have traded for just one mole, or a birthmark on her left buttock.

She would look at herself in a mirror for long spells until her misery threatened to engulf her. She was a single woman with a single thought . . . to be married and kept, comfortably. But it looked as if she was destined to stay single the rest of her life, unwanted, unclaimed, like an umbrella in the lost property office.

She sometimes wished she had as much luck as an umbrella. Perhaps if she became lost they'd put her up for sale some time, or better still, auction her off. She occasionally imagined herself, like the negro slaves of old, being auctioned off, the prize of the sale, the bidding soaring to new heights . . . sold to the wealthy, kind handsome Lord Rosedale for £125,000.

Rosalind had to live in dreamland. Reality offered nothing. Only once had she had the opportunity to be married. Long ago, when she was only 22. But then she had ambitions. Richard Lang was as plain as she, a salesman for a firm of electrical engineers, a kind man it was true, but not the man at that time for Rosalind Pertle. She had turned him down, fondly believing that better offers would arrive, that more worthy suitors would be flocking to the front door, clamouring for the hand of Miss Rosalind Pertle in marriage. But nobody had come, nobody wanting marriage, anyway. Nobody else wanting to make her his loving wife.

But she'd had plenty of the other sort. Fellows who just wanted a good time, perhaps a meal or a drink, a quick leap into bed, then home to the wife. And she was finding that the older she became, the more persistent and the more numerous were the men wanting nothing more than a sex-filled evening of her company. But this she would never stoop to. They could persist all they wanted, but they'd get nothing, not if she lived to be a hundred. But who'd want her when she was a hundred? Anyway, they could all persist off.

Now she read all the romantic novels she could get her hands on, gooey, slimy stories, the sort that couldn't possibly happen in real life, but which sent shivers running all over her body as she imagined herself the heroine, the beloved, in all the books. And her lover was always, always, Paul Newman. She adored him.

She had seen every film Paul Newman had made, and tonight had been her ninth visit to the cinema to see 'The Sting.' Fantastic, fantastic film, she thought, comparable to 'Butch Cassidy and the Sundance Kid' which she had now seen 17 times. Some people would consider it madness to see a film so many times, but she found something different, something new to demand attention in Newman, every time she saw the films. It was like seeing them on stage to Rosalind. Every show, there was some variation.

She had wanted to see the show round again this evening, but Helen, who taught art at the comprehensive, and who was also having difficulty finding just the right man, was feeling hungry and had insisted they eat at Bernelli's, almost right across the road.

It was a good time to eat, hardly anybody there, and just over an hour later they were leaving the restaurant, heading for the car park where Helen had left her six-year-old Morris Mini. They had considered going back to Rosalind's for coffee and to listen to a few records, but Helen said she felt tired and thought she would have an early night. So she dropped Rosalind off at the end of Woodland Road before setting off for home on the other side of town. She lived with her parents, and for a moment, Rosalind had had a pang of envy at her friend's good fortune. Rosalind had chosen to leave home, like many others, for the extra freedom. Now she wasn't sure she wanted it. There was a lot to be said for a home with your own parents, even if they were becoming more demanding. Still . . .

She trudged slowly up the drive, her head down, convinced she was in for a miserable night, thinking about what might have been. As she got to the front door, she looked up, starting at the sight of a policeman standing there. Her heart beat madly for a few seconds.

'Sorry miss,' said the constable. 'Did I startle you?'

'Yes, you did,' said Rosalind. She took a deep breath as she tried to regain her composure. 'What are you doing here anyway?'

Constable Connolly ignored the question. 'Are you Miss Pertle by any chance?'

'Yes, I am. Why?'

'Sergeant Newman will explain all that to you Miss. If you'd go up to your room he'll be up directly.'

'Yes, but what's happened?'

'The Sergeant will explain it all,' the constable plodded on.

'Oh for goodness sake,' said Rosalind, exasperated. But she didn't pursue the matter. She went in through the door and up to her flat. She hadn't been there more than three minutes — just enough time to take off her coat and switch on the gas fire — when a knock at the door told her the Sergeant had arrived.

The arrival of any new man into her life, however fleeting, always made Rosalind flutter a little. Where there's life there's hope, and hope was a virtue of which Rosalind Pertle had an abundance, enough for every man, woman and child in Rosedale, and Manchester, too. She glanced in the mirror, glad she still looked presentable after her day out, gave her lavish breasts a little lift, and opened the door.

Sergeant Newman pleased her, even before he said a word. Foolishly, she still judged a man on first appearance, although she was wary in her dealings with them. But he looked a gentle, thoughtful man. She smiled.

'Miss Pertle? I'm Sergeant Newman.'

'Come in Sergeant.' She stood aside, and Newman entered a room rich in clutter, rather like a junk shop, yet everything somehow blending in a strange, comforting way. Obviously she was an acquisitive woman. Books, magazines, pottery, china, vast amounts of blue glass, a wide assortment of sea shells and pebbles, records, photographs, fresh flowers, plastic flowers, one wall covered in paintings of varying sizes and shapes and subjects, a collection of dolls from various countries. He couldn't take it all in at one glance.

'Like a junk shop, isn't it?' Rosalind asked.

Newman looked at her as she closed the door. 'You've a lot of . . . things,' he said, a little at a loss to find the right word. 'I like it. And it does look lived in.'

Rosalind continued to smile. Yes, a gentle man, he'd have found some good in Jack the Ripper, she felt. 'It's perhaps with being on my own,' she tried to explain. 'I've always had the feeling I've wanted to gather things around me. Possessions somehow seem to have an exaggerated importance.' Still she smiled.

Newman coughed. 'Miss Pertle,' he said. 'You're the last person in the house to know. There's been a murder here. Last weekend, Sunday morning we believe, but not discovered until today.

Doreen Masters.'

Miss Pertle remained standing alongside a bowl of yellow, plastic crocuses. She put her head to one side, rather like a dog trying vainly to understand its master. But there was no shock in her face, not even surprise, just as if she had been told that it was raining again. She said nothing, but continued to stare at Newman with still the semblance of a smile upon her lips.

Newman decided she was not going to say anything. He took out his handkerchief, loudly blew his nose — 'Another steamer waiting to dock' his wife would have said — and continued: 'We believe it occurred last Sunday morning. Could you tell me where you were then?'

It was impossible to decide whether Miss Pertle had heard or understood a word. She stared hard at Newman, and apart from once blinking her eyes, she didn't move.

'Miss Pertle?' Newman almost shouted her name.

'I'm sorry, what were you saying?' Rosalind shook her head as if trying to clear her brain. 'Something about last Sunday.'

'Yes, what did you do last Sunday?'

'Last Sunday, last Sunday . . . let me see. I went out, I'm sure I went out. That's right, Helen and I went to Castlerigg House. I knew I'd been somewhere. And was that when the murder was committed?'

'We believe so, yes. What else do you remember of last Sunday morning? Did you get a Sunday newspaper?'

'No I didn't. I can't be bothered with Sunday papers.'

'There are some good ones,' Sergeant Newman hastened to point out.

'I'm sure you're right,' said Rosalind agreeably. 'But the popular ones are full of nothing, and the good ones, as you call them, are too big by half. Anyway, I try to fill my Sundays in other ways. I haven't time for reading newspapers.'

'Did Mr. Jones bring you one?'

'He's told you has he?' Rosalind bridled, the memory of last Sunday morning returning vividly. 'I wonder he has the gall. Yes, he brought me a paper all right. But not out of generosity I can assure you. He's just a dirty old man and he makes me sick.'

'Threw the paper at you, didn't he?'

'He's given you all the details hasn't he? Yes, he did, and I showed him the door right away. He's got some idea in his head, I think, that all single women are there for the taking. Well, he can think again. Doreen Masters might be open to offers, but not me.'

Rosalind had rambled on in her anger and for the moment had forgotten that Doreen Masters, in fact, was dead. Sergeant Newman reminded her.

'She's not open to any more offers, not since last Sunday,' he said. 'What did you mean anyway?'

'She was cheap,' Rosalind declared. 'I'm not saying she did it all the time, but she was just as like to throw her door wide open whenever a man knocked. I couldn't stand her. Not my type at all.' She went over to the fire, turned it down, and sat in the old, worn, but relaxing chair at the side. 'Do sit down, please.'

'You know,' she continued. 'Too many

men seem to think that single women, heading for spinsterhood, are ready to jump into bed at the snap of the fingers. She knew that like I do, but she egged them on. She encouraged them, and I've seen men going to her room. I've mentioned it to Mr. Rogers, but what does he say? This is their home and providing they aren't disturbing anybody else, they can do as they wish, within reason. Well, she stepped beyond reason for me.'

Newman noticed that Miss Pertle wouldn't even refer to Miss Masters by name. She obviously had disliked the woman intensely. And maybe Mr. Rogers had ulterior motives . . .

'Let us go back to last Sunday morning, Miss Pertle. Had you been out before Mr. Jones called?'

'No. I was all ready to go when he called. And as soon as I'd seen him off I left.'

'Did you hear anything at all Sunday morning?'

'No, can't say I did. Nothing out of the ordinary anyway. How was she killed?'

'Stabbed, several times.'

Rosalind made a noise that Newman interpreted as sympathy. 'No, and apart from old Jones I don't recollect seeing anybody either. Apart from Mr. Rogers. It was last Sunday, I think, when he painted the front of the house.'

'It was,' Newman confirmed. 'And other than those two men, you saw nobody.'

'No.'

'What time did you get back?'

'It was late evening. I should think getting up for ten. I'm never in a hurry to get back here. I've tried to make it a home, but it's still a lonely spot to come back to at the end of the day. Yes, about ten.'

Sergeant Newman stretched his feet out to the fire. 'You said Miss Masters had men to her room,' he said, glancing down at his watch. It was nearly ten past eight. He quickly got to his feet. 'Must get down to Mr. Rogers' place,' he said. 'Getting late. Would you come down, please, Miss Pertle? Superintendent Townley, who is in charge of the investigation, has asked for all people in the house that morning to gather in Mr. Rogers' flat. Said for eight o'clock, too, although he probably isn't back yet.'

'Yes, of course,' said Rosalind, turning off the fire and getting to her feet. 'I'll follow you down. I'll just get a cardigan.'

Newman left the room and started down the stairs. He had contacted everybody the Superintendent had mentioned, in person, and all their fingerprints had been taken. Although, for the life of him, he still couldn't see why. There was none to check them against.

He knocked on the door, which was answered immediately by Mrs. Rogers. 'Superintendent arrived yet?' he asked.

'No,' she said.

'Everybody here?'

'No, we're still two missing,' she declared.

'Two?' queried Newman. Miss Pertle he knew about. In fact, he could hear her on her way down. 'Who?'

Mrs. Rogers told him. Strange, thought Newman. That was one person he would have guaranteed to have been on time, in fact several minutes early. He felt worried, his stomach started to knot, and he felt himself go ever so slightly dizzy.

'I'd better check,' he said. 'Quickly.'

25

Superintendent Townley arrived at the home of Mrs. Edith Green, widow, sister of Carmen Rogers, at 8.15. He was hot and tired, but as excited as a six-year-old on Christmas morning. He had the answer, he knew it, but he might just as well make sure, tie up any loose ends, so to speak. In any case, Buckland was very little out of his way, only about eight miles, and it would do no harm to keep those folk waiting a little at Latrigg House.

Mrs. Green was a very attractive woman, apparently lived alone, and looked to Townley as if she could do with a bit of mature male company to make her evenings worthwhile. Still, for all he knew, she might have more men around than even Doreen Masters seemed to have had.

The house was impeccably, infuriatingly tidy. As if she kept herself fully occupied in keeping the house in order. 'I'll not sit down,' he had said to her invitation. 'I'll not keep you long.'

But he had barely had time to ask her about her sister's visit last weekend, when the telephone rang. Mrs. Green excused herself and went to answer it in the hall.

She was back in a few seconds. 'It's for you,' she said. 'A Sergeant Newman. Sounded most agitated, too.'

Townley quickly left the room, annoyed at being chased around by his Sergeant. It wouldn't do those folk any harm to wait a while. He picked up the phone.

'Newman? Look here, there's no need to go chasing me. I'll be there in quarter of an hour. Have you . . . what did you say? WHAT?' Townley's face drained of colour. The red of excitement that had been there since he left Manchester left his face as if a plug had been pulled out in his neck and the blood had all run down into his legs.

For a few seconds he listened, leaning against the wall, his free hand covering his eyes. Eventually he spoke. 'How?' he croaked. 'How did it happen?'

Newman told him. 'A scarf?' Townley repeated. 'But you were there all the time, weren't you? A man on the front door as well, and you've no idea how or when?'

The colour was returning to Townley's cheeks. But now it was the red of anger. 'Right under your nose,' he shouted. 'It's incredible. Right under your bloody nose. I don't believe it, it's just past belief. Well, you'd better keep the rest of 'em all together now. We don't want another murder. I'll be there in quarter of an hour.'

Townley hung up, his hand shaking considerably. But before he returned to Rosedale, he had to have a word with Mrs. Green. Perhaps more than just a word.

26

It was getting up for a quarter to nine when Townley stormed through the front door of Latrigg House, alive again with lights and police officers as the tireless fingers of the law picked their way through the mass of matter that might provide one shred of evidence.

Newman was waiting at the door. Townley barely, but perceptibly, hesitated in his stride as he reached the Sergeant. He looked at him, but without a word resumed his rush into the house to the scene of the second murder.

Miss Shuttleworth lay on her living room floor, lying on her side, at first glance maybe just sleeping. But around her neck was tied her own red and white woollen scarf which Superintendent Townley remembered having seen earlier in the day hanging behind the door. She had been strangled, and while Doreen Masters had clearly been dead about a week, not an hour had apparently passed since this defenceless woman's death.

'Newman,' Townley called. 'In here.' Townley went into the kitchen, followed closely by Newman, who knew exactly what was coming. He hadn't managed to get the door closed before the first question assaulted him.

'How in the world's name was this woman murdered with you in the house, and with a man at the front door, no more than 20 yards, no 10 yards, away?' Townley bawled through his anger. 'You have been here haven't you?'

Newman fidgeted. Whatever he said sounded like excuses. It was inexcusable that another murder should happen in this house, and with two policemen on hand. He lifted both arms in the air and then let them fall lifeless by his side.

'She was alive when I called to ask her to be in the Rogers' flat for eight o'clock. I saw the Rogers first, then Miss Shuttleworth. It was soon after you left, so it must have been about twenty to seven.

'I told Hart and I caught the Joneses

coming back in. Then I went to Father Johnston and Mr. James, and I suppose I got back in here about half past seven. She could have been dead then, I don't know, I didn't have any reason to call on her again. I don't see there was anything different I could have done sir. I HAD to tell everybody to be here, then I waited for Miss Pertle to come in.'

'But Newman,' Townley snorted. 'We knew, didn't we, we knew that the murderer was one of a handful of people, all being gathered together. They should have been watched, shouldn't they?'

'I couldn't watch them all at the same time sir, could I, till they were all together. And by that time, she was dead, wasn't she? And she didn't seem a likely candidate for murder anyway, did she?'

Townley took a deep breath. 'All right, all right,' he said, quietening down. 'Where did you go when you came back to the house?'

Newman scratched his nose. 'I had another word with the Rogers, they wanted to know about seating people, that sort of thing, then I went into Miss

Masters' flat again before Miss Pertle arrived. And I wouldn't think that was long — about 15 minutes. Then I went into Miss Pertle's flat and stayed there till I returned to the Rogers' apartment to see if everybody had arrived. That's when Miss Shuttleworth's non-appearance was pointed out.'

'Holy grandfather.' Townley took out a handkerchief and wiped his forehead. He blew his nose vigorously a couple of times, then looked again at Newman. 'Anybody we can eliminate from this one?' He looked and sounded weary. This shouldn't have happened. He should have told Newman of his suspicions before he left the house, put Newman on guard against the person Townley was convinced had committed these crimes.

'Nobody,' said Newman with conviction. 'Not even among the married ones. In both cases, with the Rogers and the Jones, at some time between me telling them about the meeting and the murder, they were apart. Lavatory, cup of tea, bedroom, they all moved around and there was enough time for Miss Shuttleworth to be killed, and for the murderer to return to his or her own room. After all, even for Mr. or Mrs. Jones on the top floor, how long would they need to get down here, then back upstairs. Hart says he was in his room all the time, and there is no way of checking that the outsiders went straight into the Rogers' flat. I've asked Constable Connolly about the people who came in. Do you want a word sir?'

'No, you tell me,' said Townley.

'The Joneses came back soon after you left. Miss Pertle arrived about ten to eight, with Father Johnston close behind her and Mr. James a few minutes later. Miss Pertle would have had time to call in, but Mr. and Mrs. Rogers say they have no idea how long a gap there was between Father Johnston and Mr. James. Father Johnston was first, they're sure of that, then everybody else came virtually together, the Joneses, Mr. Hart and Mr. James, with Miss Pertle the last. Why do you think Miss Shuttleworth was killed sir?'

'Obviously she knew something, something incriminating about the murderer,' returned Townley. 'The murderer couldn't have known whether she'd already told us her bit of information. But they were going to make sure anyway.'

'Has she told us anything sir, that would put a finger on any of those people next door?' questioned Newman.

Townley, who was looking at the floor, lifted his gaze to Newman's face. 'Yes, Newman, she did,' he said pointedly. 'And when she saw this particular person, I think she realised suddenly that she was face to face with Doreen Masters' murderer. But it was too late.

'Anyway, let's get in among them before there's any more blood shed,' said Townley, turning for the door. 'You did take all their finger-prints, didn't you?' he asked.

'Yes sir.'

'I mean EVERYBODY who is in that room.'

'Yes sir, I've got the lot. But what are they for? We didn't get any prints from that room.'

'Never mind for a minute, Newman,' said Townley. 'You go in the Rogers flat. I'll be in there in just one minute.'

The Superintendent and the Sergeant left the kitchen and walked back through the living room where Miss Shuttleworth lay dead. Townley averted his eyes. He couldn't face her. He felt ashamed. She shouldn't be dead, she should be sitting in that room across, ready to listen to Townley and his exposure of the murderer.

Newman went across the hall, knocked on the door, and walked straight into the Rogers' flat.

Townley walked upstairs to the first floor, and let himself into Doreen Masters' flat. He turned on the light and looked around. Incredible, he thought, two murders in the one house. He walked over to the table still bearing two coffee cups, lifted one and put it into his handkerchief. He took last week's Sunday Chronicle — the one that had been left in this room — from his pocket, tucked it under his arm, and let himself out of the room again.

With the cup in a handkerchief in one hand, and the newspaper in the other, he walked into the Rogers' living room to face Sergeant Newman and the eight people he had asked to see. One of them a double murderer!

27

Everybody, with the exception of Mrs. Rogers and Sergeant Newman, was sitting round the large oval table. A space at the top had thoughtfully been left for the Superintendent, and on the left of that, sat Ernest and Gertrude Jones. Ernest was sitting back, quiet, on the stand chair, one arm on the table, considering his finger ends, and hardly acknowledging Townley's entrance into the room. His wife was chatting noisily to Roger Rogers, who was sitting next to her, but stopped immediately Townley walked in.

Len James was sitting at the bottom of the table, talking earnestly to his friend, George Hart. Both looked up as Townley entered, but James carried right on with his conversation as if nothing had happened. Rosalind Pertle came next, pensive and almost prim, sitting with her hands neatly together in her lap. And last of all, the man who would be sitting on the Superintendent's right, Father Joseph Johnston, who looked up as Townley went into the room and never took his eye from him until he was seated next to him.

'Won't you sit down Mrs. Rogers?' said Townley as he took his seat, placing the cup wrapped in his handkerchief on the table in front of him, but putting the newspaper down the side of the carver chair, between his thigh and the chair arm.

Mrs. Rogers looked extremely nervous, unable to stay still for longer than a few seconds, shifting weight from one foot to the other or moving to the sideboard to remove an invisible piece of fluff. 'No, if you don't mind, I'll stay here,' she said. 'Would you like a drink of anything, water perhaps?' she said.

'Yes, I'd better,' said Townley. 'This looks like being a dry job.'

As Mrs. Rogers moved hastily into the kitchen, Sergeant Newman sat on the chair near the door, and took out his notebook and pencil. As he waited for his water, Townley again looked round at the seven other people at the table. As his eye caught George Hart's, Len James stopped talking, and now there was complete silence in the warm room. Mrs. Rogers returned with a glass of water which she put in front of Townley, then she returned to her spot near the door, standing at the side of Sergeant Newman. 'If anybody does want anything, you've only to say,' she said with a quick smile.

'Goodness,' thought Newman. 'She IS in a state. All of a dither poor woman.'

'As you all know,' said Townley, one quick glance around the room taking in all the inhabitants as he said those four words, 'One of your fellow residents, Miss Doreen Masters, was found dead in her room this morning. And I'm sure you're all well aware, as well, that only this evening, Miss Gladys Shuttleworth, in the room across the hall, was found strangled. Two murders in this house, and both, I believe, committed by the same person.

'Now I've called you all together here, because so much of the evidence of all of you overlaps, and because . . . ' here he hesitated as he cast his eyes once more over every person in the room . . . 'I believe it will help me to draw this matter to a satisfactory conclusion. This evening,' he said with due drama.

'Are you saying,' put in Mr. Rogers, leaning forward and staring penetratingly at Townley, 'that you think you know who killed Miss Masters and Miss Shuttleworth?'

'Yes, I do,' said Townley.

Father Johnston shifted in his seat, lifted his eyes from the mahogany table, and joined Rogers in a close scrutiny of the Superintendent.

'And if I'm not very much mistaken,' said Father Johnston in a quiet, even tone, 'you're also saying that the person who committed both those murders is in this room. Am I right?'

'You are,' said Townley, just as quietly. 'I am saying just that. The murderer of Miss Masters and Miss Shuttleworth is one of the eight people in this room.'

Townley's statement was greeted with complete silence, apart from Miss Pertle's sharp intake of breath, and an involuntary gasp from Mrs. Rogers. Mrs. Jones lifted her hands to her face and looked round the table, slowly studying every face. 'That's preposterous,' she panted.

'Is it, Mrs. Jones?' said Townley, looking at the far wall over Len James's head as he said it. Then he turned his head swiftly towards her. 'It might be preposterous,' he said. 'But it also happens to be true.'

Everybody now seemed to have got over that momentary shock that Townley's remark had given them, and they all looked round, shifty eyed, wondering, astonished.

'I'll explain,' said Townley. 'Doreen Masters, an attractive young woman with a way of her own with men, was found dead in this house this morning, stabbed to death. As far as we know she was last seen alive last Saturday night . . . by Miss Shuttleworth, who recalled that at about half past nine, Miss Masters called on her for some milk. She was dressed ready for bed, and after she left Miss Shuttleworth, that was the last she was seen of alive. At least as far as we know, because Miss Shuttleworth was quite sure that not an hour later she heard footsteps going up the stairs. And at about quarter past eleven she saw a man hurrying down the drive, a man she thought had been here visiting Miss Masters on other occasions. Now, did any of you have visitors last Saturday evening?'

'Not here, not to see us, Superintendent,' said Rogers, as he pulled at his eyebrows.

'No,' said Hart, while Miss Pertle and the Joneses simply shook their heads.

Townley continued: 'We have not been able to establish the identity of that man. Quite obviously, we would like to, although I am not attaching too much importance to this missing, mysterious, night visitor. Because we are certain the murder was committed some time on Sunday, and to be more precise, some time on the Sunday morning.

'One of you,' and here again, Townley looked all round the room before continuing, 'called on her on the Sunday morning, perhaps on the pretext of giving her a newspaper, and killed her.

'Now then. As you all know, the front door is locked at night and unlocked in the morning by Mr. Rogers, unless he's away, or somebody is out until the early hours. That didn't happen on the Saturday night. Mr. Rogers locked up as usual, and opened the door the following morning when Miss Shuttleworth was leaving for eight o'clock mass. And from that time on, he was painting at the front. Only Father Johnston here came into the house from outside that morning, and while Mr. Rogers cannot remember all the comings and goings of you inhabitants, he does KNOW that the Father was the only visitor. And as you all know, the back door is permanently barred and locked, so our murderer either came in through the front, past Mr. Rogers. Or he or she was in the building all the time.'

Once more Townley stopped to let the importance of his words sink in. Just a touch of the dramatics again. It did no harm and often paid dividends.

'Of the inhabitants, he recalls only Miss Shuttleworth and Mr. Hart going out. That's right, isn't it?' said Townley, looking at Rogers, who was still rubbing his eyebrow.

'Yes, yes,' said Rogers. 'Others might have done, but I can't remember. Not now. They're people you see all the time and it's hard to bring them to mind on a particular day a week ago.'

'He remembered Miss Shuttleworth because she was first out, going to mass, and Mr. Hart because he, too, was fairly early. Going fishing wasn't it?' Townley glared up the table at Hart.

'Yes,' grunted Hart.

'But you came back pretty soon after because you had forgotten something?'

Hart did not answer this time, so Townley pressed on. 'And while you were in here, looking for your missing flies, you, Mr. James,' here Townley moved his head slightly to his left, 'were sitting, waiting in your car, waiting for your fishing partner to return so you could get off for your day at Hard Booth reservoir?'

James looked surprised to be brought into the discussion. After all, it had nothing to do with him. He was away all day Sunday and hadn't set foot in the house. He was here, plainly, because of the mess George was getting into.

'Yes, out there on Woodland Road,' he declared. 'Didn't think he'd be long, so I waited in the car. Took longer than you thought, though, George, didn't it?' he laughed nervously.

Townley intercepted quickly. 'That's right, Mr. Hart, isn't it? You came in on your own?'

Hart moved uneasily on his chair, and unfastened the top button of his shirt. It was getting hard to breathe. He felt enclosed, stifled. 'Yes, I did,' he said. 'But I wasn't all that long,' he protested.

'And you didn't see Mr. James at all, did you, Mr. Rogers?' said Townley, turning his head again.

Rogers looked at Len James, who was beginning to blush, his face taking on a brighter and brighter red. He had been inflicted with blushing all his life, and while it didn't attack him often these days, it still affected him from time to time, and embarrassed him no end. And his face was scarlet now as Rogers looked at him.

'No,' said Rogers. 'He wasn't here. Never seen him before this evening, come to that. Complete stranger to me, and I'd know if he'd been here last Sunday, all right.'

The colour started to leave James's face, and a weak smile flitted across his mouth.

'I thought that was so,' said Townley as he unfolded his handkerchief, exposing the coffee cup to view. 'And that's why I couldn't for the life of me understand how your fingerprints, Mr. James, came to be on this cup in Miss Masters' room.'

28

The silence in the room this time was oppressive. It was impossible for ten people to be so quiet in one small room. But it wasn't a soothing quiet . . . it was ominous, the sort that precedes the storm, hanging over everywhere, ready to explode like a hydrogen bomb. The sort that could last only two or three seconds, yet feel like a whole month.

James broke the silence. He had to. 'Me?' he shrieked. 'No, not me, I wasn't anywhere near that room on Sunday. I couldn't be, could I? You said so, yourself. Sitting out in the car, then fishing. All day, weren't we George? It was late at night before we got back, then I was in the pub till closing time. Anybody'll tell you. No, not me. Must be mistaken. Can't be my fingerprints. How could it? How . . . ' James would have rambled and blustered his way on till morning if the Superintendent had let him. But Townley broke the flow.

'Now, Mr. James, I didn't say anything about Sunday, did I? I know you weren't there, don't I? No. no, it was Saturday night you were here, weren't you?'

James's panic gathered like clouds. 'Me, Saturday night, whatever makes you think that? Can't stand this house. Horrible place. I've always said that, haven't I George? Can't abide the place. Wouldn't set foot in it. And anyway, what would I want in that woman's flat? I'd no reason to be here. No there's a mistake somewhere. It's all a mistake, I don't know . . .'

'Mr. James,' said Townley firmly. 'Let's have no more. Your fingerprints are on that cup, and you were in this house last Saturday night, seeing Doreen Masters, weren't you? You were her regular boy-friend at the time and you were the last person to see her alive, weren't you?'

James looked around. Everybody was staring at him. They all suspected HIM. Even George was staring at him, a pained expression on his face. They were all looking at him, accusing, nobody saying a word. His hand brushed over his head as he pushed his chair back and got to his feet.

'What are you saying?' he cried. 'What's Saturday night matter anyway? What's Saturday night got to do with it. She was killed on Sunday, wasn't she?'

'Quite right, Mr. James,' said Townley without raising his voice. 'But this is a loose end I wanted tying up. The last person to see Doreen Masters alive. It wasn't Miss Shuttleworth at all. It was you, Mr. James, wasn't it. Your regular late call on Doreen. It was you Mr. James, wasn't it?' Townley demanded.

James bent his back and leaned forward towards Townley. 'What if it was?' he shouted. 'What if I did see her Saturday night? All right so I was here, so I did call to see her. I'd been seeing her a few weeks and I called last Saturday night. I stayed less than an hour and when I left she was still alive. I didn't kill her,' he screamed, the panic rising inside him again, welling up, just as if he were going to be sick. 'She was alive I'm telling you when I left. It wasn't me. Nothing to do with me. It was one of you lot killed her,' he said, throwing his arm in a wide arc to take in everybody in the room.

'All right Mr. James, all right, calm down,' said Townley. 'I'm glad I've cleared that up. Bothered me no end. Now I know it was you she'd been seeing recently and was with her last Saturday night. Now sit down, will you?'

'Just so long as we get that straight,' James persisted. 'I couldn't have been in this house Sunday. I was out fishing the whole time, me and George.' But he did sit down, flopping into the seat.

Newman had learned not to be surprised at anything Superintendent Townley did. But he couldn't help but wonder at this turn of events. What had made him think in the first place that James had been in the house on Saturday night, seeing Doreen Masters? There was no evidence that he knew of. Why him? The Superintendent must have been certain before he went into that pantomime with the fingerprints, and that was something of a gamble, too, for if James hadn't had coffee with the woman, he probably wouldn't have admitted he had been in the room. The crafty old devil. But where did that lead them?

Townley looked away from the exhausted Mr. James and turned his attention once more on Hart. 'That fishing expedition,' he said. 'That bothered me, you know. You're a regular fisherman, aren't you?'

'What of it?' Hart growled.

'Yet you leave your flies behind and have to return for them.'

'Now don't you get on to that again,' started Hart.

Townley kept right on going. 'I couldn't see why. If you had wanted to kill her, you could have done that before leaving for Hard Booth. But did you, in fact, genuinely forget your flies, return to the flat, and on some whim decide to knock Miss Masters up and see how your luck was running?'

'No, no, that's not right at all,' Hart cried. 'You've got it all wrong.'

'Showed her the paper, pushed her inside, couldn't get your way and killed her in a fit of jealousy,' shouted Townley over Hart's voice.

'No, I've told you,' pleaded Hart. 'I went to my room, and I was no more than 10 minutes. Oh God, not again,' he said, resting his elbows on the table, and sinking his head into his hands.

'Ten minutes,' murmured Townley. 'Now, you thought longer, Mr. James, didn't you?' he said, returning his attention to the man at the end of the table.

James hadn't been listening. He had been lost in his own thoughts, wondering how the focus of the murder case had switched to him. Everything had looked black for one horrible moment.

'Mr. James . . . '

'Eh, I'm sorry,' said James. 'What did you say?'

'Mr. Hart said he was back in the house no longer than 10 minutes looking for his flies. You thought longer, didn't you?'

'Oh yes. You must have been 25 or 30 minutes, George, you know,' he said, turning to his friend.

'Never Len. Never in this world. I was in and out in a few minutes.'

'Sorry George, old lad. At least, oh . . . 25.'

'Now look here Len.'

'What would you say, Mr. Rogers?' Townley interrupted.

'Well, like I told you before, I didn't time him. But it did SEEM longer than five minutes. It just seemed to me a long time. I don't know, though, to be fair,' he said with an apologetic air. 'I suppose it could have been 10 minutes.'

'And you Mr. Rogers.' Townley had again switched the centre of attention, leaving Hart in much the same frame of mind as James, relieved but wondering. 'You say you were at the front of the house, or in sight of the front, the whole morning. Afternoon as well, come to that.'

Rogers bristled. 'I DID say that, Superintendent, and that is exactly what happened. I was there the whole morning, and apart from going to the kitchen I didn't leave the front of the house.'

'Yes,' said Townley. 'You were painting, taking advantage of your wife being away for the weekend.'

'Like we said, she was at her sister's.'

'Was she?'

'I beg your pardon?'

'Was she . . . your wife . . . was she at her sister's?'

'Of course, she was. I told you that didn't I?'

Townley looked from Mr. Rogers to his wife, Carmen, still standing by the Sergeant, and now beginning to fidget even more nervously. 'You weren't at your sister's at the weekend, were you, Mrs. Rogers?' he said, pleadingly.

Carmen Rogers looked completely flustered now. 'What's all this got to do with anything?' she said. 'I certainly was not here Sunday morning or anywhere near here.'

'Yes, I know,' said Townley. 'But you told me you were at your sister's. But you weren't. I checked. Oh yes, I think she would have been happy to have supported your story, but not when she knew there'd been TWO murders in this house. No no, she had to tell the truth in the end. You were at a motel on the edge of Bridgeton, weren't you, with a Mr . . . '

Townley felt about for his notebook.

'Don't bother,' said Mrs. Rogers wearily. 'Mr. Don Maxwell.'

Roger Rogers looked across at his wife. 'Carmen, why . . . '

'Are you trying to say you didn't know?' put in Townley. 'Come off it, you knew all about it. Anyway, we'll leave that for the minute. And what about you Father?'

Father Johnston, dressed in collar and tie and bright red pullover, looked at the man sitting next to him.

'My turn now is it?' he demanded. 'The inquisition turns its ugly head towards the priesthood. Denounced! Ask forgiveness of your sins.'

Townley smiled slightly for the first time since he had returned to Latrigg House. 'I must say, Father, you were my first choice for this crime for quite a while. You were in the right place at just the right time, visiting this girl when she should have been out and about. Motive bothered me for a while till I found out that you frequented strip clubs, searching for the baser desires that should attack only weaklings like myself.'

'Strip club singular,' corrected Father Johnston. 'And I have explained all that.'

'Quite so,' said Townley. 'You seemed a good choice. A frustrated priest getting his kicks at the strip clubs — beg pardon, a strip club — and striking up an unusually warm friendship with a woman who doesn't even attend church. Now Sergeant Newman, you see, thought this was ridiculous, a priest suspected of murder. But like I told him . . . and I was right, too, Newman, wasn't I? . . . they ARE only flesh and blood like the rest of us. But then it all came to me in a flash.'

He looked slowly round the faces in the room. Complete, utter silence had returned. The climax was approaching, and nobody was going to miss a word.

'You see, my big mistake was in taking one big factor in this case for granted. Took it on its face value and it threw me completely on the wrong track. I should have learned through the years not to take things for granted, that things often aren't just what they seem. It's like assuming that the man driving the Rolls Royce is wealthy, or that the man with a cigar in his hand smokes. Or that the man wearing a dog collar is necessarily a minister,' he said pointedly towards Father Johnston.

'Yet I took one important piece of evidence, just like that, for granted. And it turned me in the wrong direction altogether.

'It was you, Mr. James, who put me on the right track, and I'm grateful to you. Remember, you were telling me about the Yorkshire edition of the Daily Observer. About newspapers having different editions to make sure the Yorkshire folk get Yorkshire news, and Scottish folk don't get the Cornwall racing results. Remember, Mr. James?

'Well, this evening I've been taking this a stage further. I've been to the Sunday Chronicle office, finding out all about editions, how many there are, difficulties of printing, this sort of stuff. Did you know, Newman' . . . he turned round as he addressed the Sergeant . . . 'that the Sunday Chronicle has ten different editions? Many of the pages are the same through all editions, but some change to provide local news and local sport. After all, we around here want to read about Manchester United and City and Rosedale, don't we . . . not Newcastle and Sunderland and Gateshead or anything like that.'

Townley paused a minute. Whatever is he driving at, thought Newman? What has a newspaper's editions got to do with the murder of Doreen Masters and Gladys Shuttleworth?

'And of course, printing on a big paper like the Sunday Chronicle is quite a job. The print up here in Manchester is over two million. Imagine that Newman.' Townley screwed his head round again. 'Just imagine, two million copies. Consequently they have to start printing early, and the first editions to go are for the places furthest away, like Ireland and Scotland, then the North East. And the last of all, printed for the people in the Manchester area, is rolling off in the early hours of the morning. That's right, isn't it Mr. James?'

'For sure,' said James with a puzzled expression.

'And that's where I went wrong,' said Townley. 'You see, we found a copy of last Sunday's Sunday Chronicle in Miss Master's flat. On the coffee table I think it was, wasn't it Sergeant?' Again he turned round. 'Anyway, it was this newspaper that had put me on the wrong track altogether. You see, because the Sunday paper was already in her room, on the coffee table, we ASSUMED it had been brought in on the Sunday.

'I took this newspaper,' he brought out the Sunday Chronicle and laid it alongside the cup and his handkerchief, 'with me to the Sunday Chronicle office earlier this evening. Had a very nice, illuminating chat with the Editor, who told me that the copy I was holding was a North-east edition, printed for that part of the country.'

Rogers, who had listened intently to this, couldn't resist interrupting. 'So this paper was brought down from the North-East LATER,' he exclaimed.

Townley looked at him pityingly. 'Dear

me, no, Mr. Rogers. Oh no. This newspaper was brought in here on the Saturday night before, wasn't it . . . Mr. James? I never connected the two before — the Daily Observer and the Sunday Chronicle printed in the same building, and you working casual shifts for the Chronicle, Mr. James. And you worked last Saturday night, too, didn't you, till ten o'clock? The North-East edition of the Sunday Chronicle was printed at 9.52 that night, and you were able to get a copy on your way out.'

James was on his feet again. 'You can't prove that,' he cried. 'Nothing to do with me, nothing at all. It's all out of your head, that's what it is.'

Townley shouted him down again. 'You were there, weren't you? Saturday night. You've admitted it. You left work at ten, and came straight here, didn't you? Straight up to Miss Masters' room, didn't you? And killed her?'

'No, no,' shouted James. 'It wasn't me. Not me, not me at all.' He looked round the table wildly. 'It was him,' he shouted hysterically, pointing at Hart. 'When he was back here all that time, Sunday morning. That's when it was. It was his baby she was having, his baby, not mine, and he had to shut her up.'

'Baby?' Townley cut in. 'Baby? Who said she was having a baby? I didn't. Did you, Mr. Hart?'

Hart shook his head as he stared at James. 'So that's why you kept insisting I'd been a long time looking for those flies,' he said quietly.

James was crying. He had sat down again while Townley and Hart were talking, and now he was sobbing, his hands over his face. Townley continued: 'It was you she told about the baby, wasn't it? And I shouldn't think it was the first time was it?'

James shook his head. 'She'd been pestering me for a few weeks,' he sobbed. 'Said she'd have to go away for a while and kept on about an abortion. Said I'd have to pay.' He lifted his head, and dropped his hands on the table. 'But why should it be my baby? She just didn't go with me, she had lots of men friends. It could be anybody's. Why me? Said she'd tell the wife if I didn't do it. She wouldn't shut up. Kept on and on and on about what she was going to do if I didn't pay up. She wouldn't stop. I told her to, told her what I'd do if she didn't shut up. I did warn her,' he pleaded. He started to cry again.

Townley, however, hadn't finished. 'And Miss Shuttleworth?' he said. 'She recognised you, didn't she?'

James nodded. 'She was leaving her flat just as I was coming through the front door. 'You' she said to me, and pointed at me like a witch. 'You, you're the one who was seeing Doreen.' She started to shout so I pushed her back in her room.' James was staring into space now, his eyes vacant, seeing nothing. 'She wouldn't shut up, just like Doreen. Then she started to shout. I had to stop her, I had to.'

James was sobbing heavily, his shoulders heaving, his head nodding vigorously.

'All right Sergeant,' said Townley authoritatively. 'Have him taken to the station.'

James rose meekly and obediently as

Newman steered him into the hall where two detective constables escorted him to a waiting car.

Townley, who had followed Newman into the hall, stood, his hands in his trousers pocket, a constant, satisfied smile on his face.

'Very nice,' he said. 'Nicely wrapped up.'

'Saturday night,' mused Newman. 'Never thought of Saturday night.'

'Ay, he only admitted it because he thought he was giving nothing away.'

'And because he thought you had his fingerprints on that cup.'

'Yes, a bit devious that,' agreed Townley. 'But I had to get him to admit he'd been there Saturday night. If he didn't, I had no evidence at all that he'd called here after working at the Sunday Chronicle. But when he thought we were convinced the murder happened Sunday morning, and he had a sure fire alibi for Sunday morning, he thought he was giving nothing away Saturday night.'

'Well, once he had admitted that, why didn't you grab him straight away?' asked Newman.

'Oh, just a bit of cat and mouse, you know, Newman. Cat and mouse, that's all. No harm done, eh?' he said, as he walked through the front door towards his car. He squeezed inside and looked at the time. Nearly ten minutes to ten. Not a bad day's work at all, that.

Newman walked slowly back to the house and in through the front door. He looked at Miss Shuttleworth's door before turning in at the one opposite. Everybody was still sitting, including Mrs. Rogers, all talking at the same time. Newman looked at them. The Rogers, the Joneses, Miss Pertle, Hart, Father Johnston.

'No harm done, eh, Newman?'

No . . . not much.

THE END

Other titles in the
Linford Mystery Library:

ACCOUNT SETTLED

John Russell Fearn

When scientist Rajek Quinton was pushed, screaming, down a mineshaft by Emerson Drew's hired killer, Drew and his co-conspirators Darnhome and de Brock were set to exploit Quinton's amazing invention. But he reckoned without Larry Clark of the C.I.D., and Quinton's genius. Larry, aided by Drew's secretary, Joyce Sutton, obtained the evidence needed to send Drew and his cohorts to their doom. But exactly who was Joyce Sutton? And did Quinton really die in the mud-filled pit shaft?